My Baby Shot Me Down

My Baby
Shot Me Down

blinding books

This edition of 'My Baby Shot Me Down' © 2014 Richard Penny

All poetry and prose © 2014
Clarissa Angus, Katherine Black, Maggy van Eijk, Harriet Goodale,
Deborah Hambrook, Claudine Lazar, Rachael Smart,
Ruth Starling, Alison Wassell, Laura Wilkinson

All works edited and arranged by Richard Penny,
Ruth Starling and Rachael Smart

Jacket art © 2014 Siobhan Ward

A CIP catalogue record for this title is available from the British Library

ISBN 978-0-9567-8113-0

First edition

Typeset in Baskerville by Hewer Text UK Ltd, Edinburgh
Printed and bound in Great Britain by Clays Ltd, St Ives plc

Papers used by Blinding Books are from well-managed
forests and other responsible sources

Blinding Books
6 Willow Court
Woodlands Road
Guildford GU1 1AR
www.blindingbooks.com

£1 from each copy sold to be shared equally by
Abctales and the children's charity, Railway Children

Contents

Alison Wassell

Alison Wassell is a former primary school teacher who now pays her bills by selling bottled gas whilst attempting to become a 'proper' writer. She has been longlisted, shortlisted and placed in numerous competitions.

'I Blame The Parents' was the winning story in the microfiction category of the New Writer Prose & Poetry Prizes 2012. 'Guests' was placed second in the Words With Jam Bigger Short Story Competition 2013.

Alison shares her home with her cat, Lily, who remains unimpressed by her achievements.

Gallivanting

We were the last family in the street to get a telephone. It had its own shelf; a semicircular glass and wrought iron monstrosity attached to the wall. People would be able to get hold of us now, my mother declared. Who might want to get hold of us was never specified. My parents, both only children, were middle-aged orphans before they met. There were no grandparents, aunts, uncles, cousins. None of us had any friends.

That first night, we waited, afraid to turn on the TV or radio in case the noise drowned out the ringing. We smiled nervously at one another. We were not good conversationalists. Occasionally, we glanced into the hall where the phone sat. It remained stubbornly silent. My father was the first to lose hope.

'I think I'll turn in,' he said, as he always did at 9.30. He shuffled into the kitchen to make his cocoa. My mother picked up her knitting as I remembered some homework.

The ringing startled us all. My father and I looked to my mother, as the most confident of the three of us, urgently motioning for her to answer the call.

Rising to her feet, she strode into the hallway, patting her hair as she went. With a deep breath, she lifted the receiver.

'Six three nine four nine,' she said, in a voice I had never heard before. After a long pause, she looked at the receiver and replaced it, thoroughly nonplussed.

'Wrong number,' she explained, as though she had somehow let us down.

As the phone gathered dust, it became a reminder of our oddness. Sometimes, arriving home from work, my father tossed his jacket over it. Normally obsessively tidy, my mother left it lying there.

One Saturday afternoon, as I lay on my bed staring at the ceiling, it rang. I pictured my mother wiping her hands on her apron. She chanted our number so loudly the neighbours must have heard. I listened to her listening.

'Who shall I say is calling?' she asked, in her special telephone voice. I sat up, intrigued by the thought of a phone call genuinely intended for one of us.

'Hold the line one moment, please,' she said, before scurrying up the stairs and barging into my room.

'Anne, Anne, it's for you,' she hissed, shaking my shoulder as she spoke, as though to wake me up. Tentatively, I followed her downstairs and picked up the phone.

'Hello, Anus,' said Diane Finney. Anus was what they called me at school. My parents watched from the sofa, hand in hand, smiling benignly. I smiled back.

'Hi, Diane!' I said cheerfully. Someone cackled in the background.

'We'll be waiting, on Monday,' promised Diane. I was to make sure I had my dinner-money with me. I knew what would happen if I failed to pay up.

'See you then!' I said, replacing the receiver. My parents exchanged proud glances. My mother was the first to speak.

'We won't know her from now on,' she told my father. 'She'll be out gallivanting with her friends all the time.'

My father gently pecked my cheek. 'I knew that phone was a good idea,' he said.

A Bite of an Apple

Molly knows that if she bites into the apple, something bad will happen to her. It would be like Snow White, but with no handsome prince to kiss her back to life. Eating apples away from home is on The List.

The List grows every day.

'Just one more thing,' Mummy whispers into Molly's hair as she hugs her tightly. Today's little lesson is about not playing in the big sandpit, because you never know what bad things dirty children have done in it.

Molly has apples at home, but Mummy has to peel them first because there might be germs or chemicals on the skin, and germs and chemicals are things that can make you sick. When the apple has been peeled, Mummy chops it up into tiny pieces. It takes a long time and sometimes the apple starts to go brown. Mummy has to watch while Molly eats the tiny pieces in case one gets stuck in her throat and she chokes. Lots of things can go wrong when you eat an apple.

Now, the bowl of shiny red apples sits in the middle of the circle of children at snack time. Nearly everyone has taken one. All around her, children are cheerfully biting, and none of them seem to be dying. Molly listens to them chomping and her mouth starts to water.

Edging slowly towards the bowl, her fingers close around the smallest apple, because that might be the safest one. She stares at it for a long time, turning it over in her hand. The teacher tells her to hurry up. Molly opens her mouth as wide as it will go and takes a bite.

She likes the tingly way her teeth feel as they sink into the apple. She likes the frilly edge that is left where she has bitten. Juice runs down her chin. She waits for something bad to happen. Nothing does. She takes another bite.

4

Soon, all that remains is the core. She takes out the pips and holds them in her outstretched palm. Her teacher smiles and says maybe she can plant them and an apple tree will grow. But Molly isn't allowed to plant seeds, because they have to be planted in mud, and mud is the same as dirt, which is bad for you.

The end of the day comes and the bad thing still hasn't happened. Mummy waits in the playground wearing her worried face. She holds out her hand to Molly. Molly doesn't take it because Mummy has told a big lie. She wonders how many other lies there have been.

Tomorrow, she will play in the sand. She might even take a drink from the water fountain.

On the way home, Molly walks behind her mother, keeping a distance between them. She thinks about The List and what other lies there have been. Mummy is no longer to be trusted.

King of Cliché

You never can tell what's around the corner. This was one of his favourite sayings. He had a lot of sayings. Cliché was his first language. His life was what he made it. Educated at the School of Hard Knocks, he graduated from the University of Life. He was knocked down. He rose like a phoenix from the ashes. Illness struck. He retaliated with a Positive Mental Attitude. He put up a brave fight. He won. You can't put a good man down.

He sneered at those who accepted the hand they were dealt. He punched above his weight and won the girl of his dreams. She was the apple of his eye. All's fair in love and war. He had beaten the odds. He popped the question. She said yes. She would have been a fool not to. He was worth a bob or two, though he said it himself. So what if he was no oil painting? Beauty was in the eye of the beholder.

They tied the knot, without a hitch, on a hot beach somewhere, with just a few close friends to witness the happy event. She was the blushing bride, red as a beetroot. She had caught the sun. He said a few words to his guests, sharing his pearls of wisdom. He said that love conquers all and his cup was overflowing with happiness. He was over the moon. Secretly, he was beginning to doubt his choice. The guests said, 'it couldn't have happened to a nicer couple.' He reminded his bride that all you need is love. When he sang The Way You Look Tonight, she repelled him with her purple, blotchy body. But he had no well-worn phrases with which to express his dismay, so he said nothing.

Retiring to the bridal suite, mellow and fuzzy from too much wine, they clumsily consummated their love.

Fate smiled, although not on them. She went over to the window and carefully adjusted the trajectory of the billowing curtain over to the candle that they had left unextinguished. This was what she had intended all along. You never can tell what's around the corner.

I Blame The Parents

They would be the world's best parents. No one was more qualified. They both worked with children; she was a social worker, he a teacher. They had read all the parenting books and knew when all the important milestones were supposed to happen. They even bought a special journal in which to record them. They took lots of photographs, in the beginning.

He was a beautiful baby, just the right weight and size. He had his mother's smile and his father's eyes. People envied them – the perfect little family.

He gained weight as expected. He sat, he crawled, and finally, he walked. In fact, he strode. His legs soon lost their infant chubbiness. He seemed like a little man, having somehow bypassed toddlerhood. They laughed, at first. He was obviously special, they said.

He did not speak. He did not babble. He did not say 'Mama' or 'Dada', nor did he emit any other form of baby-talk. He watched and listened. They claimed not to be worried. He would speak when he was ready, they assured each other.

They advanced in their careers. She submitted an article to a magazine on the importance of talking to your baby. It was accepted and widely well-received. She became a child-rearing guru. There was talk of a TV series.

She lectured other parents on how to bring up their children. Stimulation was important. These days, children were language impoverished. Far too often, children were addressed only when they were in trouble. They were shouted at, not spoken to.

Her husband stood by proudly, nodding along with a permanent smug smile on his lips. He gave up teaching to become her manager.

Nobody dared to mention the irony of their silent child. In fact, not many people knew. As the expert couple toured the country, spreading their message, he was cared for at home by a nanny. A carefully chosen, highly qualified nanny, obviously. If they hadn't employed her, at great cost, they'd never have been able to help others, they said. The audience would gently nod their approval.

Aged almost three, he sat up in his bath and looked around. It was on one of those rare weekends when his parents were at home.

He fixed them with a gaze that stripped them of all their child-rearing certainties. His lip curled into a sneer. Using the logic that had served them so well, they comforted each other that it must have been a playful smirk. He sighed, and shook his head.

'It appears that you have forgotten to purchase soap again,' he remarked, in perfectly enunciated tones. It was to be the first of many shortcomings that he would bring to their attention.

For once, the experts looked at each other without speaking. They had liked him better when he was silent.

Ashes

She is dry-eyed at the funeral. Later, at the wake, she passes round plates of sandwiches and slices of a cake she has baked herself. People exchange glances and clichés. She is bottling things up. It hasn't hit her yet. They wait in vain for the deluge of grief.

Her son solemnly places a ceramic monstrosity on her mantelpiece.

'So much nicer than the plastic one from the undertaker,' he says, embracing her awkwardly. 'He's still with you, Mum,' he whispers, a tremor in his voice.

With her face pressed into his jumper, she swallows the urge to laugh.

Alone, in the evening, her eyes keep returning to the urn. She shifts uncomfortably, turning away from the mantelpiece in an act of open defiance. Slipping off her shoes, she leaves them lying carelessly on the carpet. She curls her legs beneath her and reaches for the remote. For five minutes she flicks through the channels. She settles on a soap opera. She is sure she hears his tut of disgust.

Her appetite has never been better. She opens the kitchen cupboard in search of a late night snack. She gazes at the meticulously aligned tins of soup, oldest at the front, alphabetically arranged by flavour. Giggling like a schoolgirl, she reaches into the cupboard and jumbles them all, so that there is no longer any order to them. Pleased, she heats up her soup and takes it into the living room where she eats it in front of the television, slurping loudly.

When she has finished, she sticks out her tongue at the urn. She leaves the bowl unwashed in the sink.

Lying down in bed, she stretches out her arms and legs into his space. She reads into the early hours with one arm draped around the cat. Having previously been banished to his basket in the kitchen every night, he purrs his appreciation.

In the morning, she makes toast and returns to bed with it. She allows crumbs to drop onto the sheets. She showers, dresses, and leaves the house without applying make-up.

In town, she enters a shop she has never dared visit before. Ignoring the smirks of the teenaged shop assistants, she purchases her first pair of jeans.

She wears them while she cleans. Dusting the mantelpiece, she lifts the urn.

'Mutton dressed as lamb,' it sneers.

She slams it down a little too hard and a crack appears from top to bottom. She lifts the lid and peers inside. Grey dust stares back at her. She is shocked by how little remains of him.

Inserting the nozzle of the vacuum cleaner into the urn, she switches on. Her husband disappears in a brief, satisfying slurp. She replaces the urn, turning the crack to the wall. Later, she fills it with Jelly Babies.

Early on Friday, she watches from the pavement as the bins are emptied.

'Alright, love?' one of the men asks.

'Never better.' She gives him her brightest smile. She is still smiling long after the truck has driven away.

'Good riddance to bad rubbish,' she whispers.

Guests

'Your guests are here,' announces my mother, as she stands in my bedroom doorway with her hands on the shoulders of two strangers. One is shorter than the other, but otherwise they look the same. The welcoming speech I have rehearsed all afternoon drains from my mind and is replaced by my usual awkwardness in the presence of other children. My mother is smiling, but her eyes are giving me a 'Please act normally for once' look.

She is wearing make-up, which she hardly ever does. Her mouth has been inexpertly expanded to twice its normal size with too red lipstick. She no more knows how to be an adult than I know how to be nine years old.

'Ann has been looking forward to meeting you,' she tells the strangers. The smaller one sucks the end of her pigtail as the other one greedily surveys my room, taking stock of my books, toys and games. I know that something is expected of me, but I can only stare mutely as my face grows hot. There are heavy footsteps on the stairs and a man appears behind my mother.

'This must be the lovely Ann,' he says.

I have never been called lovely before. The man pushes his way into my room and holds out his hand. I wipe my damp palm on my dress and offer the wrong hand. He takes it anyway, laughing. My mother laughs too. Apologetically, she explains that I am 'a bit on the shy side'. Apologising for my shortcomings is something that she does a lot. The man bows and offers her his hand.

'Your carriage awaits, madam,' he says.

She giggles like a girl and issues me with instructions about letting the babysitter know if we need anything. Then they are gone and I am left with my guests. We stand in silence as car doors slam.

11

I have been planning this evening all week. I have even composed, in my head, the entry I will make in my news journal at school on Monday.

'My two best friends came to play at my house,' I will proudly begin. I have never had one best friend, let alone two.

On my desk there is a handwritten itinerary for our evening. At this moment, we should be settling down to a sensible board game. I had intended to let my guests choose from a selection I have taken from my shelves. Most of them, requiring more than one player, have had their shrink wrapping removed only to allow me to study the instructions. A refreshment break is scheduled for 7.30. Downstairs, the cakes I have made and clumsily decorated with our initials sit in a tin alongside an unopened bottle of squash. I blush now, as I think of them. The evening was set to conclude with me reading aloud a story I have written. My new friends were supposed to sit cross-legged on the carpet, wide-eyed with admiration, and to beg for more when I finished.

None of this, I understand, is going to happen.

It seems entirely possible that we will stand like this, staring at one another until the adults return.

The taller stranger, whose name is Christine, is the first to make a move. She wanders slowly around my room, touching things with hands that are not entirely clean. I want to shield my possessions with my body, but am too afraid to move. I smile tentatively at the shorter stranger, who is called Marie. She sticks out her tongue, then plugs her mouth with her thumb and crosses her legs, as though in urgent need of the toilet. I fear for my carpet.

Christine takes books from my shelves, glances at them and tosses them onto the bed. When she comes across one with pictures, she opens it so roughly that its spine cracks. Each time this happens I flinch. She looks at me.

12

'Does your mum make you do reading at night?' she asks, as though she feels sorry for me. I shake my head.

'Why have you got all these books, then?' she persists. I shrug. She comes closer and I smell cheese and onion crisps.

'Can you talk?' she asks. She tries to peer into my mouth, in search of my voice. I nod.

'Go on, then.' She waits, arms folded. I remember my last school report, where my teacher wrote that I had an excellent vocabulary for my age. But words only come easily when I write them down. I swallow several times as my brain searches in vain for the simplest utterance. I have begun to sweat.

Marie saves me. She removes her thumb from her mouth and clutches urgently at herself.

'Need a wee,' she informs Christine, who acts swiftly. Not bothering to ask for directions, she pushes Marie in front of her and onto the landing. She tries several doors before, just in time, she locates the bathroom. She follows Marie inside and waits while she wees, leaving the door open. When her sister has finished, she goes herself, swinging her legs and whistling as she sits on the toilet. Their knickers are grey, although they must once have been white.

'What you looking at?' she snarls, when she catches me staring.

I become suddenly engrossed in examining my fingernails. Christine doesn't flush the toilet. They fail to wash their hands.

Christine stands on her tiptoes and opens the cabinet above the sink. This is where my mother keeps her 'ladies things'. I am not allowed to touch them. Christine takes down an opened package and peers inside. She tilts it to show me the contents.

'Do you know what these are for?' she asks.

Truthfully, I shake my head. She laughs, then, to my relief, returns the packet to the cupboard and closes the door. She

13

comes close to me again, and her cheese and onion breath wafts over me as she whispers into my ear.

'When you get bigger, you bleed in your knickers.' My face must register disbelief. 'Everyone does. Even your mum.'

This is too awful to contemplate. I attempt to lead the way back to my bedroom but Christine has other ideas. She goes into my mother's room and flings herself on the bed without removing her shoes. Marie does the same. For a second, they lie on their backs, then they scramble to their feet and begin to bounce. They hold hands. I think that this must be how normal children enjoy themselves. It does not occur to me to join in. The bed creaks alarmingly.

My guests collapse in a breathless, giggling heap, their legs tangled. Christine eases herself across the bed with her elbows to look at me. She pats the bed.

'This is where your mum will do it with my dad,' she says.

I have no idea what she is talking about. She rolls her eyes up to the ceiling before turning to Marie.

'She doesn't even know what *it* is,' she tells her.

Marie titters behind her hand. Christine slides off the bed, showing her knickers as her dress rides up. She comes close and jabs her finger into my chest. I gasp and step backwards. This is the first sound she has heard me make.

'You stupid or something?' she barks.

I shake my head unconvincingly. She shoves me out of the way and strides back into my room. I watch helplessly as she opens drawers and cupboards, pulling things out and discarding them on the floor. At last, she finds what she is looking for. She pulls the clothes off Barbie and Ken and holds them up to show me. She presses them together and makes them do something that could be fighting or dancing. She makes groaning noises. Marie joins in. I look at the carpet, trying not to cry.

14

Christine gets bored, and naked Barbie and Ken are tossed aside. She sweeps things off my desk to clear a place to sit. Our itinerary for the evening flutters to the floor. I am thankful that she has not seen it. I feel her staring and reluctantly look up. She smiles in an unfriendly way.

'When your mum marries our dad, this will be our room,' she says.

There is a silence where my words are supposed to go. She continues.

'Because it's the biggest, and there are two of us. You'll have to sleep in that little room.' She gestures towards the room where the Christmas tree lives when it isn't Christmas. There is barely enough room for a bed.

'Your mum will be our mum, too,' she says. She pauses, licking her lips, and glances across at Marie, who is sucking her ponytail again. They grin conspiratorially.

'Your mum will like us best,' she says.

I can think of no reason not to believe her.

We do the staring thing again. Christine is the first to tire of it. She heads off downstairs, followed by Marie. I stay in my room. I retrieve Barbie and Ken and dress them, apologising to them in my head for their loss of dignity. Barbie gives me a cold, hard stare. I wonder if she would prefer a new life with Christine, who seems to be more her kind of girl. I tidy up as best I can, put my books back in their places on my shelves and return my dolls and games to their rightful boxes and cupboards. Someone has trodden on my plastic ruler and broken it. I put the pieces in the bin. I tear the itinerary into tiny bits and dispose of those, too. I stay sitting on the carpet with my head on my knees. It gets dark. Nobody comes to look for me.

I creep downstairs and stand in the hall, peering into the living room. Christine and Marie are on the sofa, on either side of the babysitter. They are all watching television with their feet on the coffee table. The cake tin is on the floor with its lid off, and empty cake cases are scattered around. Only Marie notices me. She sticks out her tongue again. When the adverts come on, the babysitter turns to Christine.

'What did you make of Ann?' she asks.

Christine twirls her finger at the side of her head. 'Weirdo,' she says.

The babysitter laughs. I go back upstairs.

Back in my room, I do what I always do when life gets too confusing for me. I climb into bed, pull the covers over my head, and go to sleep.

The sound of a car door slamming wakes me. The engine keeps running. There are footsteps on the drive, then the sound of a key in the front door. There is some sleepy mumbling before the door closes. The car drives away. My mother climbs the stairs.

I pretend to be asleep as she slumps on my bed. She is not fooled.

'Well, that was a bit of a disaster,' she says, laughing angrily.

I abandon my pretence and sit up. I click on my bedside light. She has wiped away the lipstick. Her eyes are red, as though she has been crying. She takes off her shoes and settles herself next to me, so I rest my head on her shoulder.

'I hated my guests,' I tell her.

'I hated their dad,' she says.

She hugs me tightly and I hug her back, pressing my face into her until I struggle to breathe. But all I can think about is the secret bleeding, and the Barbie and Ken dance that seemed more like a fight, and all the other things that I don't know. And the world is a less safe place.

Harriet Goodale

Harriett was raised in the Lincolnshire fens, where she spent her formative years reading anything with writing on and trying to befriend the birds. The heartless little gits rejected her.

Later, she moved to Peterborough to become a ne'er-do-well, where she is now living and ne'er doing well.

She has never published anything before and is very excited to be a part of this lovely anthology.

Checkmate

Emily had been in the backyard. Everything was covered in little white prickles; the weeds, the abandoned toys, the broken chairs. Even the dog poos. Emily showed them to teddy, her breath flaming from her mouth like dragon's smoke. She found that the prickles were not sharp. In fact, you could run your finger along them and ruin them just like that. But they were cold. There was a big, black bird on the fence. It looked at her and then it flew off. Emily went inside.

'You see, babe, she's the spitting image of you.' Emily found herself seized by the shoulders and hustled over to the settee, where slumped the flabby carcass of her mother's boyfriend. Confused, she looked toward her mother, who had dragged her there. Cigarette smoke scalded her eyes and throat. Her mother's face was empty. Its rabid expression frightened Emily, and she began to cry.

'Oh, shut up, will yer. Look, Craig-babe, she's got your nose.' A spider-like hand snatched Emily's chin and yanked her head aside. She felt Craig's gaze, searching, probing her face, and she wanted to howl, to tear at her skin and run away. She looked at the scratches on the door, which were like blades of long grass. There was a chip in the paint that looked just like a butterfly.

'I'll get a test, you'll see. That cunt will never see her again.'

The envelope – in understated brown – gave itself away. Carla tore it open with greedy, shaking hands, an animal sneer spreading slowly across her face as she devoured its contents. After reading it several times, she ground her cigarette into the ashtray and threw the letter down on the table, leaning back in her chair to shout upstairs.

'Craig. Guess what. Emily's yours.' And she collapsed into the mirthless laughter of a carrion-bird.

*   *   *

'I told you, I was seeing Craig the whole time. She ain't yours, Stuart.' Carla stretched the syllables of his name with a mocking tongue and winked at Craig.

'Please, Carla.' The tinny voice spilling from the speakerphone cracked in two. 'Please, I don't care. My mum and dad don't care. Please, just let us carry on like before. We love her.'

'I ain't having you seein' her anymore, alright? You can pick Liam and Josie up tomorrow as normal. But you're not having Emily. She's Craig's now. She's always been Craig's. And if you make any trouble, you'll never see any of 'em again.' A dark, vertical line slowly materialised between Carla's finely plucked eyebrows. She took a long pull on her cigarette, hung up the phone, and laughed smoke into Craig's face.

Emily was in the front room playing dolls with Josie, when her mother's voice leapt from the kitchen and struck her like a blow.

'Emily. Get in here.'

She dropped the doll as if it were scalding hot. A familiar terror scuttled from her belly to her ribcage, fluttering and scrabbling in her chest as her feet carried her toward the kitchen. Carla and Craig were seated at the table. Emily paused at the doorway, her body rigid with fear. Craig's gaze made her itch; her mother's face had that vacant look again. When Carla finally spoke, her voice was soft, caressing, like the smoke that danced from her lips with every word.

'Come in here, darlin'. We need to have a little chat.'

Emily stood motionless on the living room carpet, clutching teddy by a threadbare arm. A strange lump had risen in her throat and now squatted like a toad behind her tongue. Outside, a car horn beeped.

'Emily, put Josie's trainers on. Liam, hurry up, yer dad's waiting.'

Emily stumbled over to her little sister and began to pull on her shoes. The velcro straps swam before her eyes. Josie kicked her legs and giggled, excited to be going to her daddy's. Liam stood by the door, pressing his fist to his mouth and staring miserably at the floor.

'Mum. If Emily can't go, I'm not going neither.'

Emily's head snapped upright. Liam lived for his weekends with dad.

'Don't fuck me about, Liam. Craig is Emily's dad. She stays here with us now.'

'But Nana and Grandad . . .' Carla sprang from her seat and caught Liam by a skinny arm, shaking him back and forth like a dog with a rat. Josie began to wail.

'Don't you fucking talk back to me. You can go now, or never see your dad again. You think I want that cunt in my life? Do you? I do this for your benefit, not mine. Now fuck off out of my sight.'

Carla pushed Liam away and returned to her seat at the kitchen table. Liam leant back against the wall, kneading his fists into his eye sockets as his breath rasped in his throat. Josie, perceiving that something was wrong, clung to Emily and mewed bitterly. Emily could take no more. She buried her face in Josie's soft curls and began to keen like a wounded animal. Her little heart throbbed painfully; the room seemed to spin around her. Emily's five years on earth had been loaded with pain and fear, but nothing could have prepared her for this. Her daddy was her only refuge. Daddy loved her.

'Emily, shut that fucking noise right now.' Her mother's voice pelted her like gunfire and she knew she had to stop, but the tears came by themselves and would not relent.

Letting go of Josie, she pressed her forehead to the floor, fighting to suppress her sobs 'til only a whimper was audible. A tiny, helpless voice mingled with her tears and soaked into the carpet.

'Daddy.'

Outside, the horn beeped again. Liam looked at his two little sisters huddled on the floor, then toward the front door. Silent tears coursed down his cheeks. He felt an urge to run to his mother, grab her by the hair and punch her, punch her, punch her 'til her nose bled and she cried for mercy. Craig too. If he was only a bit bigger, he would've taken them both on.

'Liam, you got five seconds to get out that door, or I'll tell yer dad to fuck off and never come back. Five . . .'

Liam knelt beside his sisters and put his mouth to Emily's ear.

'I'm sorry, Ems. Don't worry, Dad won't let 'em. He'll do something, I promise.'

'Four . . .'

Liam put his arms around Josie and lifted her. She let out a squeal, kicking her legs and reaching for Emily. Emily remained a tight little ball of grief, her wet face pressed hard into the carpet.

'Three. Two.'

The front door slammed, and Emily was alone.

Josie wailed all the way to the car. Father and son were silent as together they installed her in the car seat. Her wailing subsided to little hiccoughing sobs as she started to feel safer in Daddy's car. Liam dropped into the passenger seat with the sigh of an old, old man, tipped his head back and closed his eyes. His face was still wet with tears.

'Dad. Please do something.'

'There's nothing I can do, Liam. Craig is Emily's dad. Your mum's got the papers to prove it. If I make a noise she'll cut me out completely.' Stuart's voice splintered. 'I can't lose you all.'

Stuart started up the car. As they pulled away, their eyes were drawn irresistibly back to the house. Pressed against the front room window was a small, white face.

Shall We

The corrugated plastic roof rattles
with rain, and this pleases me.
In particular, the occasional metallic
ping, as a lump of scrap is struck
in just the right place for music.
Forged and cast with care for some
forgotten purpose, now it lays dismembered,
obsolete and without function.
Rats and robins shelter within.
The rain pelts itself harder and
faster in a burst of spite;
'Notice me.'
We could walk out in it, you and I.
Out of town, where the fields sprawl,
where you can hear the earth drink the water.
We could creep under the hedge
and curl up like foxes.
Shivering and sodden
we could dissolve together.
Dead leaves and rabbit holes and spiders
Cold hands and slick skin and hot breath
Away from here.

We'll Meet Again

I thought I saw yer today. I'd been up town, to get some dinners from Iceland. It gets harder every time; everybody bargin' about, pushin' an shovin' – I allus seem to be in the way.

By the time I sat down at the bus stop I was tired out. I dumped me bags on the floor, wheezin' like an old broken bagpipe. Sometimes I'm glad you can't see me now. It was her hair that caught me eye; a tumblin' fountain a polished jet, just like yours. Aye, she were the spittin' image a you. She were standin' with a group a mates, smokin' an' gigglin'. It didn't suit her. I'm glad you never smoked. She turned my way and looked right at me wi' these big, dark eyes – well, me heart leapt in me throat an' I were twenty year old again, gazin' at you through the dancehall fug and tellin' meself you'd never dance wi' the likes a me. It were Wilkes that persuaded me to ask yer.

"G'won," he kept on sayin', "she can only say no. You g'won, lad. Ask her."

An' ain't I glad I did. You smiled right at me – I tell yer now me heart were doin' the jitterbug in me chest when ah looked in them eyes a yours. The band struck up 'I'm Nobody's Baby', you never said nowt, just put yer little hand in mine an' away we went. By, you were a nifty little mover. The gal were singin',

"Hey, somebody hear my plea, and take a chance with me, 'cause I'm nobody's baby, now . . ."

Oh an' you looked at me wi' yer eyes shinin' an' a little smile jus' curlin' that rosebud mouth a yours, an' I knew right then I wanted you for me own. You were such a little thing, you had on that em'rald-green dress that set off yer skin an' hair jus' so. Wi' me hand on yer waist I felt like a king, like there were only me an' you in the whole place. There was no way I'd let any other feller dance wi' yer after that, an' you only had eyes for me. I remember lookin' up an' seein' Wilkes stood at the bar, grinnin' an' givin' me the thumbs-up. We were allus like that when one of us caught a nice gal, but this time I felt offended. I didn't want nobody lookin' at yer, smirkin', like.

By the time I were sent away to Italy wi' the Grenadier Guards, I were a married man, wi' yer picture in me wallet. We were so in love, we didn't want to leave nothin' to chance. What if I never came back? Ah, leavin you were such a wrench, I still feel it pullin' on me heart when ah think of it. How we clung together on that platform. How I held yer little face in me hands, wiped yer tears wi' me thumbs, but more came as fast as I could wipe 'em away. Me eyes stung; I had a lump like an egg lodged in me throat. You were so afraid I'd never come back, an' I couldn't bear the thought a you workin' the land all winter, such a little thing, with our baby curled up inside yer. I took a last look into them lovely eyes, an' promised yer we'd meet again, just like in the song.

The war raged, so many good lads killed. Innocents, country lads like meself, sent into that monstrous machine, never to return. Some a me mates took up wi' local gals, an' right nice some of 'em were, too, but I only had eyes for you. They'd go off at nights, drinkin' an' lookin' for a good time, aye they laughed at me, sittin in camp wi' me photograph an' me dreams. I started writin' yer poetry. Loada tripe it was, but it made me feel better. No point describin' the horror of it all, didn't want to worry yer pretty head, an' besides, it'd never have got past the censor. But I did enjoy sendin' me poems. Jus' to let you know I was still there, still lovin' you, waitin' to come back to you an' hold yer in me arms. I never got a reply, but I carried on sendin' 'em all the same.

Yer due-date were loomin', an' it were all I could think of. How I wished that bloody war would end, how I fretted an' dreamed an' hoped. Then the letter came. It were just before

Christmas, an' we were all homesick as hell. I opened it wi' shakin' hands. Were you alright? Did yer still love me? Was it a girl or a boy? It was yer sister. You were dead. You'd caught the 'flu early November, out workin' the fields. You'd died, after eight weeks' ailin', an' the baby wi' yer. So sorry, yer sister wrote, to write such news. She'd wanted to write when you were ill, but you'd said no, not to worry me. Said I 'ad enough on me plate. You'd kept an' cherished all me poems, she wrote, read 'em every day. Right 'til the day you died an' you were so weak she 'ad to read em to yer. You died clutchin' 'em to yer breast.

After that I were a broken man. All I wanted were to join yer up there, you an' our baby. All around me, fine young men were dyin' left, right an' centre. But for some reason, I never got me wish, no matter how many risks I took. I earnt medals fer bravery, but it weren't bravery really, it were a death-wish. I courted death as ardently as I'd courted you, but it just weren't to be. The war ended an' home we came, but I felt no relief, no joy. Just numb inside. At night I dreamt of you, an' me brothers who never made it home. All me life yer ghosts have haunted me. I'm not complainin' like, yer memory is dearer to me than life itself, but I never really lived after that. Another seventy-odd years I've plodded along. I can hardly believe it's been so long.

I'm not sayin' it's all been doom an' gloom, na, life's been alright, in a quiet sorta way. I worked in the foundry over forty years, made some good friends, had some good times. 'Yer daft,' they'd say, 'yer still young, marry again, 'ave a family.' I went out wi' a few gals, but it never felt right. Mebbe 'cause I weren't there by yer side when yer passed, never went to the funeral. Somehow I never really felt like you were gone. I went to yer grave, stood a long while, jus' starin at the inscription.

'Edith Gaskell'

25

'1923 – 1944'

Still it didn't really sink in. It were jus' a stone wi' yer name on. Last time I saw you, we'd held each other so tight; I'd kissed you, tasted yer tears, promised you we'd meet again. You were so warm an' sweet an' alive. I never met another gal who could hold a torch to you. You were me one an' only sweetheart. Now yer dog-eared little photograph sits on the mantel in a frame. It's all I got left a yer. It's how I talk to yer.

So I'm sittin there wi' me carrier-bags, lookin at this gal, an' she's the spit a you. She holds me gaze a moment, an' I can feel me face breakin' into a big stupid grin. I'm under a spell, all kinds a stupidness runnin' through me mind, about reincarnation an' suchlike. Me mouth silently sounds out yer name,

'Edie!'

But just like that, she breaks the spell. Her little rosebud mouth takes an ugly shape, an' she spits at me.

'What the fuckaya starin' at, ya dirty old perv!?'

Her friends huddle round her, glarin' over at me, an' I can hear 'em mutterin' amongst 'emselves,

'Dirty old bastard.'

'Fuckin' nonce.'

'Mucky old git.'

Me ears are hot wi' shame an' I stare at the floor like a peepin' tom been caught out. I can feel the disapprovin' stares of other bystanders, an' I know they're all thinkin' the same thing. It's a relief to me when the bus pulls up an' ah shuffle into the queue. Yer little double doesn't get on, an' I'm glad. I got a funny feelin' in me chest – a tight feelin', like when we parted at the station. All the journey home, all I can think of is you.

When I get back to me flat, I shove me poxy microwave dinners-for-one in the freezer, an' stick the record player on. No need to change the record; I know what's on it, an' it's all I need to hear.

Droppin' into me chair, I close me eyes an' listen to Vera Lynn, promisin' me the one thing I've dreamt of for the last seventy years.

'We'll meet again,
  don't know where,
  don't know when –
  but I know
  we'll meet again,
  some sunny day.'

I am your oyster lover

So here we are again – another verbal beating.
You fling your poison darts with perfect aim,
master of your game you pierce my aching heart
with putrid insults that could bring the coldest tart
to tears of shame, casually slaughtering my soul
with caustic words, forgetting them immediately
upon utterance, assuming that I'll do the same.

But I'm sorry, my mind just
doesn't work that way.
They lodge like birdshot,
deep within my skull,
each and every
nasty
little
word
you say,
for mournful dissection and
analysis at a later date.

It's not deliberate, it's just unfortunate.
I don't store it up, just to throw it all
back in your face some day. But there in my
head, your words they stay. Lurking and malignant,
merging and linking, coalescing together to form a
dark and tender tumour, that throbs and needles
when you whisper words of love, hisses doubts when
you wrap your arms around me.
I never guessed, when I first came to you, that
we could ever come to this. Never thought that
every day you'd seek a new way to thrust a knife
between my ribs, stabbing and twisting until

something within me rips. I gave everything I
had to give. It wasn't much, just a meagre life,
but I gave wholeheartedly and without reserve,
thinking it so much less than you deserved.

You have torn my love to tatters. It remains
and always will, but now it's mixed with grief
and sadness, tainted by your true colours,
causing me to gaze vacantly over your shoulder
when you pull me closer. And yes I have grown
colder, for I have unpinned my heart from my sleeve
and tucked it deep where you cannot stain it. I hide
my self-worth away, that you can no longer maim it.

It's true that I've known worse, and no, you've
never raised your hand. But nothing's ever hurt
the way your callous insults can. So I fold myself
inside, armadillo-style. With every hand-grenade
you throw, my armour thickens. I am not the same.
When your poison's in full flow, my soul no longer
sickens. I am your oyster lover; I cannot be opened.
Never again will you lay eyes upon the tarnished
pearl that bears your name. Not for you, nor any other,
will my shell ever be broken.
My heart is closed, and it will not be eaten.

Gaps in Concrete

Darkness never falls here,
just stumbles gracelessly into
a murky soup that's less than light.
The firmament is veiled tonight,
by a film of vapour tainted sickly
yellow like acid bile, retched up
when there is nothing left to vomit.

A television lies face-down in the alley,
beaten and left for dead, bleeding glass.
Silent vigil is kept by dismembered
items of MDF furniture, a stained
mattress, and a lonely plastic shoe,
forever severed from its partner.

The birds never fall silent here,
but their song is different, somehow.
Desperate. Uneasy roost is broken by
angry voices, smashing glass, as different
tribes and different cultures clash. Knives
flash and sirens wail, whilst up above, doves
nestle and fidget and comfort each other,
murmur sweet nothings in mournful refrain,
again and again.

But over in the vacant plot, thistles and
nettles and grasses fight, Buddleja and
Elder lay claim on split concrete, docks
and dandelions assert their right.
This is where Fox brings his kill, to
devour in derelict garages, amid
split bin-bags and used needles and

accumulated detritus of a city
that has eaten its fill.
And then some.

As I creep with due caution through
neglected thickets of dog-rose and
blackthorn, adorned with ragged
carrier-bags that flutter forlorn like
captured flags, it occurs to me that if,
by some calamity, we are erased from
this planet like misplaced pencil strokes,
it would only be a matter of months,
'til our filthy existence became no more
than the remnant of a bad dream,
a sleeping frown upon the face of the earth.

And I think of the joy,
the sweet relief I would feel,
upon waking from such a nightmare as this.

Laura Wilkinson

Laura is a writer, reader, wife and mother to ginger boys. After hedonistic years in Manchester and London, she moved to Brighton. As well as writing fiction, she works as an editor for literary consultancy, Cornerstones.

Laura has published short stories in magazines, digital media and anthologies. Her third novel, the recently published *Public Battles, Private Wars,* is the story of a young miner's wife in 1984; of friends and rivals, loving and fighting, and being the best you can be.

For more, visit laura-wilkinson.co.uk or follow her on Twitter @ScorpioScribble.

Buried

I sit at the table stirring my coffee. A letter rests against a framed photograph on the mantelpiece. Curled, shaky handwriting in blue ink. Sender: Mrs Roberts, Mynydd Isa, North Wales. The heavy air warns of a summer of sultry afternoons and sleepless nights. She has made contact again.

In the summer of '76 the school holidays dragged on and on, sticky days and weeks melted like chocolate into an unrecognisable shape.

There were water fights galore on the estate; we were reckless with our supply. Standpipes were for those in the south, bans a thing of the future. Prides of glistening children gathered to wreak revenge on bad tempered, out-of-work dads, using bike pumps and washing-up liquid bottles. It was a favour to the men, who were bored and boiling, sitting on pigeon-grey ground blowing smoke rings into the scorched air. They played along, hollering, and threatening to belt us if they caught us, which they never did.

It was the year I waved goodbye to girlhood. I was sixteen and in many ways still childish. Friends on the cusp of womanhood looked down on me through eyelashes heavy with mascara, plucked eyebrows arched. I didn't care. That summer I met Kaz Roberts. I knew who I was and where I was going. A long, long way from the estate.

There's another photograph on the mantelpiece, next to the one propping up the letter. In it, I'm sitting on a beach in Greece; a wide-brimmed hat casts a shadow over my face.

At twenty-two, I'd forgotten almost everything about being sixteen – everything except meeting Kaz. Sweet, my arse. I hated it. I left memories of under-developed breasts, bad haircuts and home-made clothes where they belonged;

34

rotting in the corner of a dilapidated town hall, former host to Saturday night discos and other remnants of a decade sent scuttling to the sewers with the furious yell of punk.

Having packed in my crummy job as a recruitment consultant, I travelled around the Greek islands with two university mates. Frances and Juliet were brunettes and as beautiful as fresh dates. Glossy and smooth, they radiated confidence. I watched the men, who longed to squeeze them, check their firmness and sink their teeth into the girls' ripe, juicy flesh. I felt like a Cox's Pippin wedged between exotic fruits.

On our last night before the journey back to Britain, we went to our favourite haunt; a family-run bar on the golden sands of Laganas. As we climbed the steps from the beach, I noticed a woman sitting at the bar in a backless sundress. I thought of Kaz Roberts. There was something about the woman's form, the contours of her back, the distinctive mole on her left shoulder blade. It transported me to the long, hot summer of 1976, the walk to the White Gates at Nercwys, and Kaz Roberts's perfect back.

Another endless, baking day. Children milled about on the scrubby grass, which the council laughingly called a park. We were restless, so a small gang of us decided to go exploring. We walked the three miles to the White Gates in the unforgiving sun and, like the Pied Piper, we picked up more kids along the way.

As we approached the main road leading out of town, I saw Kaz Roberts and three of her cronies leaning against the wall of the big, posh house that marked the end of our crummy council estate. Kaz had left school a couple of summers earlier. She'd a reputation as a hard-nut after putting a chisel through a rival's palm during a woodwork lesson, slapping a teacher and kicking several sorts of shit out of numerous other girls. Everyone expected her to be pregnant or on remand within weeks of leaving, but she confounded us all by getting a job at Boots the Chemist, on the make-up counter, no less. She was very pretty. We were petrified of her and we admired her for reasons only teenagers understood.

'Where are you lot going?' she spat, between drags on her Embassy.

No one spoke in the long seconds that passed as she looked us all up and down.

'The little kids want to go to the White Gates,' I mumbled. I barely lifted my head from a prayer position.

Kaz surveyed our ragged crew. She took another draw on her ciggie, dropped it and twisted her foot on the concrete, hard and deliberate. I was surprised her flip-flops didn't burst into flames.

'We'll come too,' she replied. 'It's Gail, isn't it?'

Kaz led the way; we fell in behind her like a platoon, and I took the opportunity to study her. She wore a tatty halter-neck top and shorts cut from old jeans. Her skin was the colour of a *Caramac* bar: golden and creamy. Her back was broad and velvety, left shoulder blade highlighted by a large beauty spot. She was lovely. She looked like a model from a *Top of the Pops* album cover; sexy, available, and slightly cheap. I imagined her in a fur bikini – like Raquel Welch in *One Million Years BC* – and if you ignored the swearing, and the strange Welsh-Liverpudlian accent of our area, and honed in on the timbre of her voice, it was languorous and smooth. I wanted to be wrapped in it. Her bleached, flicked hair formed a halo around her head.

No one spoke much; the heat drained energy. I answered when spoken to, and by the time we finally approached the gates, we had been more or less silent for a quarter of an hour.

The gates were disappointing, but the setting was beautiful – a field spotted with thistles and daisies, a river ambling through it. My feet were killing me. I wanted to dangle them in the water. I told the others to walk on to the ruins of the house without me.

'I'll see you on the way back,' I said.

Kaz hovered like a hornet. I stumbled to the river bank and sat down. I looked at her feet. She plonked herself down beside me and announced that she couldn't be fagged to walk any further either.

'You want one,' she said, waving a cigarette packet, her eyes boring into mine. I shook my head. She tipped the box, tapped the base, then gripped a cigarette with her sticky, glossy lips and eased it into position. A brush of her finger against a lighter and the cigarette was burning. I watched her lips contract and relax as she dragged. She held the cigarette between her middle and ring fingers, high up, almost touching her fingernails, which were coated in an electric blue lacquer. The veneer was chipped in places, and as the cigarette smoke twirled into the sky it looked like vapours escaping from her varnish. She didn't seem to inhale. She rolled the smoke around her mouth and held it there, captive, before releasing it with an exaggerated sigh. I wished I could smoke without choking.

I kicked off my sandals and lowered my feet into the river. Water slid through my toes, caressing my aching soles and licking my ankles. I put my hands behind my back, locked my elbows and tipped my head to the sky. My hair brushed against the grass. The sun burned through my eyelids, and when I lifted my head I was dizzy. I could make out the outline of Kaz's body, but I couldn't see her features.

'Your hair must be a right pain to look after, being so long and all that.'

'Not really,' I replied, plucking a daisy from the bank. 'I hate the colour.'

'You get called names cos of it?'

37

'Sometimes, but I don't care.' The heat was making me reckless.

'I'd care about stuff like that. It's good you don't.' She lit another cigarette.

'How's the job?' I said.

'Alright. Bit boring.'

'My mum says jobs in retail are worth holding on to. Solid, you know, secure. With potential for career progression.' I mimicked my mum's tones.

She looked at me as if I were mad. 'Is that what you want to do? Work in a shop? I thought you were clever.'

'It'd make my mum happy,' I said, rolling my eyes. 'Steady job, steady life . . .'

'Steady bloke.'

Phillip, a friend of my brother's, had asked me out at the beginning of the holiday. I'd refused. He might have been desperate, but I wasn't.

Kaz stared at me, serious. 'You got anyone?'

'Nope. You?'

'Not really.'

Her gaze unsettled me, and I stared down at my feet, and hers, watching them change shape under the water's surface. She moved her left foot towards my right.

'I've got huge feet, haven't I?' she said. As if to prove her point, she shifted closer and tucked her foot underneath mine, her toes popping out like children peeping over a wall, wide-eyed and playful. Legs entwined, feet circling, flesh on watery flesh, calf muscle against calf muscle. She shaved her legs; I felt the stubble pricking my flesh as we played foot-tag in the water.

She fell back on the coarse grass, her head in the cradle of her hands. I followed suit and we lay there, elbow to elbow, until the others returned.

*   *   *

38

Gentle Mediterranean waves lapped against the shore.

'How did you know it was me?' Kaz sipped her Ouzo.

'I recognised the mole. Your mark.'

'Everyone calls me Karen now.'

'I'm known as Gee,' I replied, and she laughed.

'They good mates?' She nodded at Frances and Juliet. 'You gonna invite them over?'

'I'd rather have you to myself.'

She smiled and raised her glass. 'I recognised you straight away. You've not changed.'

'The hair?'

'The freckles.'

'You look great.' And she did. I took a drink and stole a glance at her feet. They were wrapped in leather sandals, gladiator-style, with the thongs crossed up her calves. Her toenails were painted a fashionable pink.

We didn't talk about the past. She told me about her travels around Greece; I told her about mine. We talked as if we'd known each other all our lives, and, in a way, we had.

I went to the toilet. As I returned along the unlit path running beside the bar, Kaz approached me. She pushed me against the wall and brushed her mouth along mine. The roof of my mouth sparked; a weakening in my spine and a rush to my scalp. Her touch was confident and strong; her pelvis pushed into the soft flesh of my stomach as we kissed. Heat flushed my breast, neck, cheeks, and, feeling boneless, I was close to collapse when she pulled me through the bar and onto the beach. She threw me onto the damp sand and sat astride my thighs and gripped my wrists, forcing my arms above my head.

'I love your freckles. I love your hair. The length, the colour – like leaves in autumn.'

I looked into her eyes and then closed mine quickly. The sky was too black and the stars too bright. I felt her breath on my neck; warm and sensual. The touch of her lips on my breasts.

Later, in her room, I picked sand from between her toes. I ran my tongue up her inside leg until she howled with pleasure. I tickled her back as I rubbed in cocoa butter cream and etched my name onto her skin with my fingernail.

She ran her fingers through my hair, scratching my scalp so hard it hurt, and then buried her face in my hair. She was breathing so heavily I wondered if she was crying.

'No, I'm breathing you in. I want to remember your smell, the feel of your hair. I don't want to forget.'

'You don't have to.'

'You'll do well for yourself,' she said, lying back on the bed. 'You're going places, not like me. Mine's a small life. Always will be. This is running away for a while – I'll have to go back.'

'No one has to do anything these days.'

'People like me do,' she sighed. 'And anyway, what else can I do? I've got a bloke waiting for me back home. At least I think I have.'

Her hands climbed up my hair, pulling me onto my back once more. We stared at the ceiling, white plaster speckled with the blood of flattened mosquitoes.

'Kiss me,' I said, and she did. Again and again.

In the morning I was shy. I wondered what I would tell Juliet and Frances. I remembered their shocked faces when I approached Kaz. The way they took in her cheap clothes and haircut. The condescension lurking beneath their smiles when I did, finally, introduce her. 'How lovely to meet you. Gee simply never talks about her old friends.'

I laughed when Kaz said, 'We should meet again – during a long, hot summer.'

We swapped telephone numbers, written on used ferry tickets from Piraeus.

*   *   *

40

Kaz called in July '96. For a woman who left school without qualifications, she was enterprising and resourceful. I'd moved five, maybe six times. I kept in touch with no one from Wales. I'd lost touch with Juliet and Frances, though 'lost touch' gives the wrong impression; I disappeared and rein-vented myself, again.

But Kaz traced me.

'Dead easy,' she said. She wanted to meet.

'I've met someone,' I said.

'What's he like?'

'She. She's lovely. Her name's Hermia.'

'Posh. Always said you'd do well!'

'She calls me her 'bit of rough'.'

Kaz laughed, but I wondered what she expected from our meeting. I was in love with Hermia and I didn't want to mess up.

It was hot that year; Camden Town sizzled. It felt like the most exciting place on earth, looking to the future, and I had no time for my past.

When I got to The World's End, I was twenty minutes late. I'd fretted over what to wear. I wanted to look good, but not provocative, nothing too revealing, which wasn't easy given the heat. The pub was packed. I hovered by the door scan-ning the crowd.

Kaz was sitting at the bar and I was shocked at the change in her appearance. Her hair was still long, but instead of rich brown it was a poorly dyed red. The evening light caught the grey at the roots, the lines fanning from her eyes, the yellowed teeth as she smiled at a man sitting across from her. I thought of the money I spent at expensive hairdressers and boutiques. Her dress was dated, too tight and unflattering across her chest. She wasn't wearing a bra and needed to. She was no longer the Amazonian goddess of my youth. She was a poor, uneducated woman, prematurely middle-aged. I imagined hairs sprouting from her mole. She looked like a hooker. Dread washed over me at the thought of someone I knew seeing me with her and I could not stop myself turning and racing out of the bar.

I look to the mantelpiece, to Hermia's photograph and the letter resting against it. Another ten years pass before my eyes; career, mortgage, an adopted boy.

Kaz.

I hope she's happy, that life is good to her.

I tear open the letter, stomach spinning. It isn't Kaz, but her mother. Of course. How could Kaz be a *Mrs* Roberts?

Dear Gail,

This is Mrs Jean Roberts of Gwernaffield. You might remember my daughter Karen. She was a few years older than you at school. I'm writing to tell you that Karen died just over a year ago. I would have told you earlier but I didn't know how much you meant to Karen until I read her diaries and it took me a long time before I could do this. She had ovarian cancer and though she was brave and fought hard, it got her in the end. Karen wrote such a lot about you, Gail, in her diaries. She described you with long auburn hair and she said you were the only person who knew the real Kaz Roberts.

Since that summer afternoon in '76, when we lay on the parched grass, legs entwined in the brook, her imprint has remained in my soul. Like a fossil. Buried, but always there. Her gift; my future. In that moment, she changed my life.

I weep at the table; the dense air presses down on me. It will be a long, hot summer.

The Whispering Wall

The first time Lucile heard the crying, it was the dead of a summer's afternoon.

She assumed it was her next-door neighbour's son until she remembered they were on holiday. When she told Edward that evening, he smiled and shook his head.

'You're imagining it. Either that or the bloody woman's invited some of her friends to use the house while she's away,' he said, returning to *The Independent*.

'We'd hear them if there were visitors, wouldn't we, Eddy?'

He peered over the pages, eyes bloodshot, and said, 'Probably. I can't imagine any of her lot being quiet. But look, Lulu, it's all in your head. Not surprising after everything you've been through.'

'We've been through,' she whispered. 'Anyway, I rather like her.'

'You need to rest more, darling,' he said, before disappearing behind his newspaper again. 'You're overdoing it.'

Lucile wondered how she could possibly be overdoing it. She hadn't worked in six months, not since she'd been ill, and she'd done nothing in the house. The move had been Edward's idea. She needed somewhere quieter, somewhere to build a future, he'd said. Highgate was perfect and the house backed onto the cemetery – a place they both loved. Had loved. Edward rarely went there nowadays.

Later, Lucile lay in bed staring at the walls, an open, unread book resting on her chest. She could hear only Edward, the soft whistle of his out-breath. She closed the novel, rolled over and watched him sleep. Flat on his back, the duvet pulled up to his hips, sweat beaded on his forehead, his lips fell apart and this slackness gave him the appearance of youth. She longed to stroke the fleshy rise of his belly, to feel his skin against hers. She reached out, and then stopped. Her hand hovered over his chest, the hairs tickling her palms. Sighing, Lucile turned over and closed her eyes; he would be furious if she woke him up.

She woke to the sound of whimpering. The room was clothed in shadow. Startled, she sat up. She held her breath and strained to hear more. There was a long pause, then it came again, louder this time. Lucile pulled the duvet aside and climbed out of bed, careful not to disturb Edward. She stood still for a moment, her feet welcoming the cool of the bare floorboards. A breeze wafted round her ankles and she realised that the bathroom window had been left open. She went to close it, looking out over the gardens first, half-expecting to see Samantha and her boy.

Crazy. It's the middle of the night. Of course they're not there. They're on holiday, you fool, she thought.

As she crept back to the bedroom, it came again; the sound of crying from the far wall. The party wall. A deep wardrobe covered its entire length; not quite walk-in, but large enough for the estate agent to mention it a few times. Lucile slid open the heavy doors. Dresses, jackets, shirts and suits swayed from side to side. She parted the clothes and leaned in. Nothing. She waited, but the crying had stopped. The only sound was the rustling of plastic-covered shirts, fresh from the dry cleaners.

As she prepared Edward's breakfast, Lucile decided not to mention the crying again. He would only think she was making a fuss. Since his recent promotion, he'd been more distant than ever.

He sat down at the breakfast bar smelling of aftershave. Lucile didn't recognise the fragrance and was about to ask what it was when Edward said, 'Lulu darling, I'm afraid I have to go away again. One of Iain's clients, his mother's had another episode. Needs twenty-four hour care, at least until he gets a home sorted.'

'God, how awful, poor Iain. And Teri. Do pass on my best wishes.'

'I will, sweetheart. Bloody inconsiderate disease, Alzheimer's.'

Lucile smiled at his feeble attempt to make light of Iain's pain.

He came up behind her and squeezed her shoulders. 'Sorry I didn't mention it last night. I didn't want to upset you after that crying business. You'll be alright, won't you, darling?'

'Yes, yes, of course. I'll be fine. Are you going anywhere exciting?' She turned the bacon in the grill.

'God, no. Brussels, then The Hague – bloody boring places. I'll bring you something lovely.' He gave her shoulders another quick squeeze and sat down again.

'Why don't you get some of your old friends over while I'm away? It'd do you good.'

She passed him a breakfast of eggs, bacon and hash browns, and said, 'I'm not sure if I'm ready for that. I don't know if I can face the questions. What I'm up to, why the move, why we haven't got children yet.'

'None of their bloody business, that's what you tell them. You're trying to forget, move on.'

I don't want to forget, she thought. 'Calm down. It's not as if they've actually said anything. I'm nervous, that's all.'

'Well, there's no need to be. Look, darling, I've got to shoot. Sorry about the food. Have a good day.' And with that, he was gone.

Another eleven, twelve hours to fill before he returned home. Lucile took a leisurely bath and drifted into the village. It was such a contrast to Chelsea. Intimate, higgledy-piggledy, leafy. It was a beautiful day and everywhere she went there were babies in buggies, mothers with small children on trikes, women with swollen bellies and happy, smiling faces. She turned round and walked to the cemetery.

It was quiet, hot and sultry. Flowers bowed in the heat on the graves of the recently departed, twigs snapped underfoot as Lucile inched into the heart of the graveyard. She sought respite in the shade of the Circle of Lebanon and walked it until she was dizzy, and, though she fought against it, she found herself drawn to the tombs and headstones of children. Precious, stolen children immortalised in stone etchings and watched over by angels.

Ten days passed before Lucile heard the crying again. It was night-time and Edward was away. She sat in the wardrobe for two hours or more, waiting and listening, an ear pressed against the wall. A mewling, at first plaintive and lonely, built to a demanding, angry howl before shrinking into exhausted sobbing. It sounded like a boy.

In the morning, Lucile knocked on the peeling paintwork of her neighbour's front door. There was no answer. They had not returned from holiday.

For three nights Lucile rose and waited for the child, but he did not come.

Edward walked into the kitchen clutching half a dozen white lilies. 'Christ, Lulu, are you alright? You look terrible.'

He offered the gift. The cloying scent of her favourite flowers hung in the close air. Lost for words, Lucile looked at him, silent.

'What's happened?' he asked, fiddling with his keys, avoiding her eyes.

She turned her back to him as she lied. 'Nothing. I've not been sleeping, that's all.'

'Are you out of pills? Ask the doctor for more. I could do with a few myself. I'm bushed.'

Edward certainly slept deeply. He retired to bed early and was asleep by the time Lucile emerged from the bathroom in a lace-trimmed baby doll nightdress. Disappointed, she exchanged the frills for cotton pyjamas. Brushing her hands over her wide hips and full breasts, she felt betrayed by the body which had promised so much.

That night, the boy returned. Lucile heard him crying through the wall, though his sobs were barely louder than a whisper. She sat on the floor and pressed her face and palms against the wallpaper. She could see him now. Blonde and pink with blue eyes and fleshy thighs. How she longed to hold him. To cuddle him, to comfort him.

For five nights he came, and then he stopped. Weeks went by and still the neighbours hadn't returned. Edward was away on another business trip and Lucile was lonelier than ever. It hurt. She sat in the wardrobe for hours, day and night, waiting for the boy.

Then, late one afternoon, he came. His voice was faint, as if he were at the end of a long tunnel and not the other side of a few bricks. Lucile huddled in the corner, listening. Here, the wallpaper was loose, bubbling, almost peeling. She picked at it with her fingernails and tore away a large strip to reveal another layer beneath. A dated pattern of blue and grey stripes, it was harder to remove. Lucile went to the kitchen for a knife.

She scraped at the wall. Away came another layer to reveal large pink flowers, roses or carnations, set in a yellowing background of stems, thorns and frayed leaves. Another layer came away, then another, and another, until she came to a dusty, faded print: sandy teddy bears with burgundy ribbons round their necks. A nursery paper.

She pushed her nose to the wall and sniffed. It smelt of talcum powder and camomile. As she pulled away, she saw the pencil mark; a squiggle, like a child's handwriting, the message concealed by a layer of paper still attached to the wall.

The sun had set but Lucile was sweating. She clambered out of the wardrobe and raced downstairs, across the garden and into the shed. Amidst the chaos, she retrieved a torch, a scraper and a toolbox. Heart racing, she returned to the bedroom and began throwing clothes and shoes out of the wardrobe. Armed with a wet sponge and metal scraper, Lucile attacked the remaining wallpaper. It slipped off with ease. She followed the childish letters, jagged and scrawling. At first, she couldn't decipher the message, but she persevered.

Help me. Help mummy help.

The crying filled her head. She tore at the teddy bears until her fingers were raw, exposing the brickwork beneath. She grabbed a hammer from the toolbox and chipped away at the crumbling red bricks. The crying continued, louder and louder. In despair, she threw down the hammer and bolted out of the house back to the shed for the pickaxe.

She knocked along the wall. It sounded hollow. There was a cavity; she was sure of it. She hauled up the pickaxe and swung it at the wall. Bricks cracked and fell to the floor in a cloud of dust. Coughing and spluttering, she pulled at the stone, blood trickling from her battered hands. The crying grew louder and more desperate until she could bear it no longer. Then, quite suddenly, it stopped.

Lucile was staring at the remains of a child, entombed in the cavity wall. Unafraid, she reached out a shredded finger to touch the skull. She felt an unmistakable flutter in her belly. The stirrings of a child. An unborn child. She looked at her bloodied hands and tried to remember the last time she had bled. It was weeks ago. Many weeks ago. Before the wall began to whisper.

Rachael Smart

Rachael Smart is a social worker from Nottingham with a thing about words. Her work has appeared in Litro, Cease, Cows and Prole Poetry and Prose.

She is hopelessly addicted to the writer's website, ABCtales, and likes to write in floppy notebooks with a blunt pencil. Visit her at smartrachael.wordpress

Little Lost Reds

My tongue – always
too crude for your tastes.
Bottomless kisses;
awash with slime and sticky.
I muddied your waters,
left oil smears on your ethics.
My vulva was bitter sours when
all you wanted was sweet.

The one thing you gave me,
a threat – you'd more to lose;
your wife, a child. No matter, though,
when I was slammed on top
or beneath you. Chop off my head,
let it roll. You may as well now
this woman's listed
for execution.

You'll go down with me.

Look into my neck scrag,
beyond its gore, climb down.
No. Deeper, slink into the
swamp of my belly. You'll hear
heart thrusts, a pulse snarl to judder
bone. Lower, still. Submerge yourself
in soft ribbon red, shrouds of
muscle, woman's pink.
In this wild pit, blood pushes,
I drum with come what may.

A wolf inhabits here,
in these guts, her haunches furled
in membranes pale. Keep watch from
your reddened shade; a stranger
enters swift, the nick of his looped knife,
a rip over being. Man, do not look away.
Hush now. Hear the voiceless
screams of her withdrawal; the wolf
keens a lament for little lost reds.
You too, now, are slick with this blood.

This time the carnage goes unhidden;
lamb juice and boysenberries, the
dusky oaks of Syrah. Once upon a time
stains, the shouldn't have
been but was – no more.
I'll scour up the ruby spillage.

Before this, you told me that
I was vulgar – in a good way.
You said that I talk from
between my legs.

I do now.

Patriarchy

Don't like your face? Get a new one. Lower your ears, inflate your lips, inject your forehead, nuke the fat off your thighs. Don't eat, you greedy tart. Make yourself retch. Deprive yourself of nutrients until your ribs rack, no back fat, tight butt, pose like a slut. Vomit after a good meal, purge that excess. Cut your breasts open and stuff them full of saline. Rip your pubic hair off, revert to a pre-pubescent girl. That'll sustain his flaccid cock. Wear black widows on your eyes. Glue acrylic to your fingers. Tattoo in new boundaries. Bleach it, inject it, hammer it, starve it. Make yourself smaller, shrink violet, breathe in, stop talking, don't take up too much room. 'The daft cow, she's gone too far. Looks like a famished dog, all big eyes, big teeth. Nice abs but she's got no tit.'

In early gestation? Await livid stretch marks. Hoover-bag cankles. Track the A52 in vein across swollen breasts. Try not to raid the fridge, sob with hunger. 'She's banging the weight on. Looks like she's smuggled a planet. Pregnant women don't really do it for me.' Nine months of perpetual sleep awake. A frog-legs staccato on a full moon stomach. Anal fissures. Bleeding gums. Short of breath. Round ligament pain. Acne. Whatever you do, don't have pain relief in labour. Pack healthy snacks in your hospital bag. Get a Brazilian wax, the vagina's centre-stage. Get your hair done for the big day. Pack your video camera.

Got contractions? Don't complain, you're only 2cms dilated. No pain relief until you're at least 6cms. Real women have natural births. Do what's best for baby. Try not to scream, it frightens your husband. Push when you're told. Push now, ready or not. Oops, too soon, split like a peach. Congratulations, a baby girl! Wet the baby's head. German beer and strip clubs. 'She still looks pregnant.' Real mothers breastfeed. Breasts are for babies, not men. Grit your teeth when milk pulses. A baby with a steel mouth, poor latch. Don't give up. Expect agony, mastitis, cracked areola, feeding problems. Most natural thing in the world. Formula's for fakes. Don't bleat over spilt milk. Every agony strips calories. Keep going, Momma. Forget doggy style; your purple gut sways like a used airbag. Put out early or he'll lose interest, surgery or not. 'It's like flinging a welly up an alley.' Exercise after six weeks. Stop sobbing blood and fluid, you leaky rig.

Getting older? Cast a glance at men walking on spring streets. Eyes lollop in their heads like rabid cows, sweating over teenage girls' arses. Go home to tuck their daughters in to bed. Threaten to strangle any boy who exploits her and masturbate watching Hot Virgin Girls Having Sex. 'Well, they ask for it.' Unless it's his daughter. 'Nice girls don't dress like that, get changed or you're bloody grounded.' 'My wife doesn't understand me anymore. She's let herself go. I only stay with her because of the kids. You're everything she's not. Need to see you.'

Yellow Cows

He wants to touch me –
but won't. Nobody could see us
behind closed doors, the timing
mellow as the hunter's moon.
Then his boneless line;
'It's for the best.'

He breaks out into a plum
night, his doorstep babble
velvet-tongued as lavender.
No matter that I wanted to climb
inside him, wear him like wolfskin.
He leaves me with a magma fever
I'm off my giddy head,
volatile from banned touch,
the itch inside; a mockery.

I didn't sleep for days,
in wake of wanting him.
Sleep-lag made my belly ache,
to taste again, the jagged edge of dreams,
float in twilights of the senseless.
My nights; spent dreaming
about dreaming.

It may have been insufferable
had I not seen male faces
in the bedroom door.
Gangs of them, concealed
in woody growth-rings,
knot-limbed. I heard their heavy pants,
eyes a bulge; stunned bullocks

watching my squirm of open legs,
fingers dipped inside.

Phantom scents of man milk twitched
above my bed, tastes of pistachio nut
and bleach hung in my throat.
Across the curtain bustle, a
montage of livestock
crept. Silhouettes; a Hessian cow,
and single-horned goat, each
milked behind an iron gate.
The fabric swirls drenched
milk from pensile teats.

My grit-eyes squeaked on the
close. The bed; its habitat
pile of dark funk – only turning
comrade when plummy dark lost
out to luminous hues of
mustard.

Declining to watch another sky light
under blankets soft as beef,
I shake myself tame. Outside,
yellow murmurs in the street.
Breathing in, I drive fast
between car and bus –
ignite a heart jolt to keep
my wanton hips attached.

Tissue Atlas

David wants to know everything about you. Even the ugly things. You say it's definitely more weighted towards the ugly and he tells you that ugly could never put him off. So, you take off your clothes, drawing your arms in close to insulate your goose-pimpled, bare skin from the dawn frost. You smoke a cigarette and then you show David your story in scars.

Two Woodlice on Forehead

People used to call you Calamity Jane as a child, after that accident-prone wench in the cowboy musical. Rubber band legs, too. You were injured so often that it lost impact. The first time you bust your head from running around a square coffee table in the lounge, arms held out behind you, humming the low drone of a huge bumblebee. You forgot to buzz when you cracked your head on the table corner. Skin opened up wide, a gash that wouldn't close, and your world turned cherry red with abstract black shapes. Your mother held a cool, wet dishcloth firmly on your head to stem the blood flow on the way to the hospital. In broken English, the driver kept saying that he wouldn't waiver the soiling charges just because you were little.

In the Children's Department, they had a huge wooden elephant slide with a den underneath. You hid inside it and imagined living in that hidey-hole stomach in dusty Kenya, with the sun, always hot, on your head. They used butterfly clips to pinch the flaps together. You tore the incision open again that same afternoon by tumbling down two garden steps in your pink fur-edged slippers. Social workers came to your house; it was just procedure, to check up on your mother's care. During their visit, they observed you tripping over your own long monkey feet and commended your mum's high supervision levels. After they'd gone, your mother held you close to her Estee Lauder Youth Dew skin and she told you that the most painful thing she'd experienced was her love for you and your sister. She said she couldn't show you the scar because it's 'too deep inside here' and she knocked on her full chest.

You and your sister were playing at your neighbour's house when you bust the other side of your head. The elderly man had asked you to hurry into the kitchen to his wife and ask her what was for his dinner. Running through the hallway, much too fast, you gashed your head on the door frame. Back in the lounge, he was sexually assaulting your sister. The neighbours came to see your parents later; they stood far back from the front door as they apologised stiffly. They were so sorry that your accident had happened in their care. Nobody mentioned the other thing.

A Straight Road, Lower Stomach
Whilst Princess Diana was getting married, you were having a hernia operation. The street outside the hospital was bursting with crowds waving banners in blue, white and red whilst you were unconscious. A boy ate Tandoori chicken on the ward when you emerged from the anaesthetic and it looked unnaturally red. It reminded you of your insides, where the stranger's hands had been. You couldn't walk the day after. It felt like being reborn because you had to learn how to use your legs all over again, putting one in front of the other. The scar scabbed over into a tempting brown woody track. Your sister reminded you for weeks that hands had rummaged inside you and she started calling you Puppet Girl.

Orange Skin for Lungs
Pneumonia almost killed you nine times in childhood. At infant school, you were off sick for six months suffering

chest-related infections. Your mother treated you at home and when you were delirious with fever, your hallucinations took you flying up to the cream-cracked ceiling. It was only centimetres away, you actually touched it, marvelling at the cool emulsion, and then you stood up there, looking down on your own brown nest of tangled hair and long white nightdress; a skeletal body. What a thin girl, you thought, before you flew off again just like Peter Pan. People close to death don't remember much.

In assembly, the children prayed that you would pull through by the love of God. Teachers came to look at you. Doctors visited daily, tapping their cold metal at broken lungs. When consultants look at your x-rays, even now, they shake their head in solemn pity. Dr Sulphanez always told you your lungs were like looking at orange peel glossy-side up, pitted and pocked from diseases and thick with dirty scars.

A Figure Eight on Shin
It was the tip of August, the air thick as glue. There was no shampoo left, so your sister used a good slug of washing-up liquid mixed with almond oil from the kitchen cupboard. She carried it upstairs in a gravy jug. Washing at opposite ends of the bath, the suds made shapes along your dips and crevices. You watched your sister make a rich lather to shave her legs, then drew the blade across foam, clearing a snow path to reveal the clean, sparse land of Spring. 'Your turn,' she'd said. You didn't tell her you were frightened of using the blade or that the tapered black hairs were your protection. Instead, you dragged way too hard and upended the razor on one side. It carved a deep gouge, the tissues inside pink and speckled. She called you butter-fingers as she put pressure onto the blood flow, held hard onto the sting with a frothy puff of cotton wool. From then

on, there was an eight on your shin. Hairs have never grown there since.

Years later, when the telephone shrieked at the night's hush, when your mother screamed on the gag of fatal news, when your sister's accident translated as murder, when you wondered if her bike wheels had spun for one final revolution, like they do in the films, as she lay crookedly beside them. When your precious sister was covered in all that soft red road dust, you grew to love that scar too fiercely. You love it, even now, because it was when she still had breath, when her eyes saw the same sights as yours, because her fingers touched inside the pulpy hole before it knitted closed, the old skin shedding, before the edges grew anew, neat and never to be healed.

One Pound Coin on Right Forearm
You were missing something at comprehensive school and your head rattled with bones. Your detachment was too tempting for Rebecca McLennan not to pick on. When she tossed her brick of ice cream to you in the lunch hall, yellow as hole-punched mouse cheese, she said you looked like you needed a good meal. You mistook her cat eyes for warmth. You admitted that you loved it when the ice cream mixed with the fruit cocktail syrup.

Later, in the shit-reeking toilets, two girls named Frances and Anne sat on your thin legs. Mocking your budget shoes, they singed the shoelaces down to a frayed tassel. Rebecca sat at the top end of you and sprayed Sure anti-perspirant deodorant in one place on your pinned-down forearm, giving you white ice burns that seared. A golden pound coin grew there on the skin, the pus souring gold. The hospital treated you for first-degree burns. You still had your bandage on when you jumped Rebecca. She was retying her ponytail in the same shit-reeking toilets. You sent buried anger far into

59

her surprised face, denting her head against the lip of the grimy porcelain sink. As her thin arms batted at the rancid air in a playful kitten style, you tried not to think about your older sister's hands; the room you'd both shared, your body cupped up in her big sister's arms in your squeaky old bed.

A Smirk, 1" from the Vaginal Entrance

You lost your virginity to a boy from the library. Desperate to join the normal ranks, you drank a bottle of red wine and invited him to your flat. You made him risotto with basil and fresh crimson tomatoes, the pulpy pips implanted in your back teeth. Carefully, you lit candles on the balcony that made the hot air seem to melt. He ate in silence. The waxing moon made milk puddles on the black reflections of the River Trent. There were five of him by the time you served your tiramisu and his Roman nose looked less linear, his lips looking plumper with every warm gulp of alcoholic faith. He was quiet and dull and thankful, so you gave him brandy to try to turn him into someone, something livelier, to ignite a fire in his sensible belly. You didn't quite mean to turn him into that, though.

When he kissed you, he poked his cold tongue between your lips. You accepted it, an oily slug pushed deep inside and as he pushed it further still, you held onto your heave because he seemed a nice boy. He was quiet, after all. He'd told you he went mountain biking and he liked to read Shelley. When he carried you to the sofa, you imagined you were a romantic, some naked sylph in a leather-bound book. The quiet boy's eyes had been half-closed, but then he'd bitten you. He tore at your knickers. You watched a bluebottle soar over his shoulder, circling above the mess of you. He forced the hardness in and steered it through you, a metal stake that pierced your centre. You told him again and again that you'd ripped apart but he hadn't stopped, he'd ridden

60

on your vacant bones. You bled for weeks and had to stand up permanently; you remember how hard you cried when you peed. The hospital gave you two sutures and a ticking off for not seeking medical treatment earlier.

Treble Clef on Left Ankle
You were getting ready for a colleague's 21st when Tulk smashed a lava lamp against the bedroom wall because he didn't want you to go. The glass shell blitzed orange bomb debris across the carpet. Plasma splattered the cowl neck of your new black dress, line-pressed on a coat hanger at the open window. Your dress danced at you, a sudden breeze ruffled life into its crushed silk, shaping its bodice and skirt full and proud – it shimmied you a salsa as though it had already got away. Rose, the elderly neighbour, was looking up at your window from her yard when you looked down. She raised a bent finger at you that day, the crippled hand of sisterhood that saved you much later. You didn't go out that night, either. Tulk was distraught when he saw the blood from your cut ankles, wet and slippery. You laughed about it weeks later, when neon nuggets of plastic lava turned up in your Jimmy Choo's. The shards felt cool as molten ashes. That scar is still thick, swirling its musical note across bone.

Now that you are right down to your ankle, you are all storied out. You give David a theatrical 'Ta-Da!' and announce loudly, 'The End.' You curl up your body like a shrimp and spoon up behind him, his cotton sheets across you, with their scent of butter and nutmeg.

David is crying without making any sound. It's maddening when people cry like that. The pillow is salt-stained, his pink face wet. Stretching out in his squashy bed, you tell him not to cry because scars are proof of pain; survival of the fittest. Scars are a good thing. You say anything to stop his deflated face, those big eyes that have swollen into puffy slits. He runs his fingertips over your stomach. He tells you that out of all of your scars, the smirk has upset him the most. You tell David that he has disappointed you, deeply, because it should have been the figure eight.

Convulsing the Storm

It's all about the wind out there,
the vicious way it wrings you out,
makes parachutes of your Victorian style coat,
whips your hair up, string lashes at faces
drags you up with it – flying, whirls you
higher, upper and over, over and greater,
past Yale locked windows, a slam into purple roofs,
umbrella outside-in, across chimney tops,
you're nutting off wet tiles, losing soffits and fascias,
brick bumping skull slumping tile smashing,
nails grappling, straw clutching.

See how it won't put you down, won't let you go,
whisks you, scrambles you, reduces you, not so cocky now,
curled up double, braving it; jaw set, shoulders squared,
mince eyed, clamp jawed, a chimney seizure,
wind gurner hunch backer roof thrasher
It's a small world   down there
clinging on   holding fast   ride it out
weather it   storm-electric-gale-hag
lying there lying stiff lying on your side
See the way it folds you, ruffles you,
not so much carries you as whisks you,
launches you, hurls you, rips the senses from you.

Tuppences

I don't like the word 'vagina' because it's an ugly word. It has three unnecessary syllables when it's a one-syllable reality: loose, tight, in, out, bleed, birth, life, hole, gape. 'Penis' is not my favourite word, either. It doesn't possess quite enough syllables to express: 'invasion, thrusting, short-lived, shoot and fire, seed disseminator, chafing, non committal, wandering or Who's the Daddy.' I definitely prefer plain simple old cock.

But those words are anatomy. When it comes to children's worlds, their parents' intentions seem wobblier than the top tier on a Rowntree's jelly. My child is three years old and every pre-schooler I know describes their genitals with names or objects. Forgive my confusion, but am I missing something large and fish-scented here? I call a knee a knee because it is in fact a knee. My face is my face. But my friend's daughter, Jenny, aged three, has a face, two feet and a Mary. Mary is her vagina. Mary is also her Irish great-aunt, long deceased, with a penchant for Scrabble. Amelia, aged four, has a tuppence; a former United Kingdom bronze coin to pee from. Millie has a front-bottom. Not surprisingly, her front bottom doesn't eject poo like her back bottom; it jets out wee. When Millie was asked to sit down on her bottom in the pre-school garden, she alarmed teachers by lying front-down on the new seedling bed. Perhaps the dual words confused her. Tamara, aged 5, has a 'flower' without petals or colours or pretty smells. She prefers flowers she can pick. When she asks her mum why it doesn't look like a tulip, her mum tells her to stop looking for petals because it is 'dirty.'

Christopher, aged three, has a snake that will grow up to be a python, apparently. His father calls it a 'trouser-snake' but said he is not to use that word at pre-school because only Justin Timberlake is allowed to talk about big snakes, unless they're real ones in the jungle, and only David Bellamy knows all about that. Maxwell uses the word 'willy' for his penis. Willy is Maxwell's best friend's dog. The dog growls sometimes and Maxwell thinks that his genitals will eventually look like a German Shepherd with buck teeth sticking out of his piss-hole. Willy the dog is really hairy and sometimes runs wild. That's not so far off the mark, genetically speaking.

Jennie's got a Tinkerbell. Now, this is where it all starts to go wrong. Jennie was shovelling in her fish fingers and chips at the dinner table and casually told her mum that her little friend Tommy had been playing with her Tinkerbell when he last visited. One telephone call, two parental showdowns and three week's worth of vicious playground gossip later, it was confirmed that Tommy had only put a new pair of wings on Jennie's doll.

My son uses the words 'penis' and 'vagina' for genitals. Last week, his pre-school teacher contacted me. She was concerned that a child of three was using clinical words for genitals in a children's environment. It was confusing all the other children, you see, because they use different names, you see, and could I discuss it with him, make him use softer words, something more appropriate because 'private parts' are really rather secret, aren't they? I thanked her for her time and sat by the telephone, thinking that with adults like that, in a society like ours, who needs fucking enemies?

The Art of Pysanky

Seeing him unexpectedly gave me a sickening.
Lice-eyes on the slorm, all over me, our past
burst through raggedy-edged. Metres apart –
yet his gaze smothered me across the barest of air.

Bindings still slung around my neck; years of washing-line
ligature, the black tongue wags, hidden stains that surface wash
after wash; after. Old laundry: vintage baskets of girl thoughts,
sugared imaginings, freshly whipped from a still small
mind that shimmered.

He's just some bent-beaked Croat now, features obsolete
beneath a geriatric mask, lugging his wife on wheels. Their tyre lines
rut the paths, maiming saplings, make trenches in the mower's
shagpiles. Flint skies gob phlegm on his orthopaedic shoes,

as he moves a foot after a foot after a foot,
that same dilatory caution; always his Saviour.
Eggs vibrate on her lap, precarious things
that hump at their box: twelve waxing moons –

mucky whites, plume-smeared,
their minute feathered barbs tremble
so, the cracks glistening
where albumen seeps.

II

Her back was always turned
to us; a kitchen sink silhouette
boring eyes from ungraded potatoes,
the quick metal grin of her paring knife,

66

nicking at skin until they were all eyeless,
a mutual blinding.

The art of Pysanky; sketching out Ukraine on
cold-boiled maps, histories drawn in wax,
etchings shine out folktales in lacy designs.
How they glowed: incandescent in my hot cupped hands
in shades I'd never seen, giving colour to his ideas
as he blotted it from mine.

How slowly he dug out my infancy.
Curve-nailed fingers twisting at my neck,
rooting on my scalp, a trail of beeswax, cooling tight on
my newly grown skin, then his weight, dying my insides
in shades of ovum white.

The still small got lost, met with a rising
force and silence. My souvenir egg dropped – it broke –
on the edge of the walnut piano, falling
sharply, faster – faster into wet.
Shiny globs and shell-debris,
shards of it, smithereens on a paisley rug.
I hadn't realised the insides were fluid.

As he sponged up the gunk, he said: Remember that
white signifies the blank page of your future
and even as he said it:
mine was blown apart.

Ruth Starling

Ruth has written non-fiction professionally for many years, on topics as diverse as wartime propaganda and the Carry On films. She is a serial blogger, artist and photographer, with an interest in neuroscience.

Recently, she wrote her first short story in a dentist's waiting room and has found her voice as an author of fiction and poetry, posting regularly on ABCtales.com as Canonette and publishing free verse on her blog, Ephemeris.

Sid

'Right. Don't answer the door. Don't answer the phone. We'll be gone a couple of hours.'

They're always longer.

'Alright, Dad.'

'I mean it.'

I'm nine years old. I never answer the phone or the door. There's really no need for him to say this.

'Why's he allowed to go?' I ask, nodding towards Nigel, my younger brother. I hate staying in this new flat on my own.

'Because he looks innocent. He'll come in handy.'

My Dad has spent the last half an hour scanning the classified ads in the local newspaper. He rolls it up and tucks it under his arm.

'We're off to see a man about a dog and then we'll chase this advert up,' he tells me.

I know there's no point arguing. This happens most weekends when Dad has access to me and my brother.

The front door slams and I switch the television on. World of Sport. Boring. I hate Saturdays – Dickie Davies and those ladies typing noisily in the background. I like the wrestling, though. Perhaps there will be some later. Big Daddy, Giant Haystacks and my favourite, Kendo Nagasaki. I leave ITV on with the sound turned down, just in case.

I pace the strange, stark rooms, scared to look too closely at their contents, terrified that there will be a rap at the door or that the phone will ring. I know why I'm not allowed to answer them – because it could be the police. That's why Dad and his girlfriend have moved again.

I didn't like the last place above the launderette, anyway. It was grey and cold and there was a stain on the wall where Dad's girlfriend, Dawn, threw her curry at him. The

70

neighbour's dogs were the best thing about it – two huge, slobbering Rottweilers who could devour a whole packet of Rich Tea biscuits in seconds. It was a keen but fleeting pleasure to watch them eat.

In the kitchen, I survey the empty fridge with dismay. There's never anything to eat here. I apprehensively select a packet of crisps from the cupboard. They are disappointingly soft and stale, but I gulp them down anyway in hungry handfuls.

I creep into the living room, across to the long glass case that sits on the floor next to the television. I settle down flat on my stomach. Inside nestles the smooth, coiled form of an Indian Python. I tap the glass but Sid, Dad's pet snake, never responds. He is beautiful, with his glistening brown blotched skin, but very boring company.

'Murderer!' I spit bitterly at him.

I hate him.

I liked Sid at first, especially when I was allowed to hold him. I would wrap him around my wrist like a living bracelet and enjoy his supple movements. Later, though, I discovered what it is he likes to eat; pretty, pink-eyed, white mice. Dad takes great delight in dangling the poor creatures by their tails and dropping them in front of Sid as an offering. It is always more than I can bear and I run screaming to the bathroom, locking myself in until it is all over.

Tired of creepy Sid, I settle myself down on the sofa and watch TV. Eventually, Dad returns with Dawn and Nigel. My brother looks tired but the adults are twitching with excitement. They exchange a conspiratorial look and burst out laughing.

Dad holds up a cardboard box, very pleased with himself. He offers it out to me and I peek at the small, furry rodent within. For a second, I dare to hope that the dear, sweet, little hamster might be a gift for me.

'Free to a good home!' Dad guffaws, slapping my brother on the back. 'You did well, you little liar, promising to take good care of him. That was a nice touch.'

My heart clenches painfully with the realisation that the hamster is destined to be Sid's dinner.

I'll never learn.

I run, sobbing, to the bathroom.

i-Spy

'How was Thunder Thighs today?' Claire asks, trying to make her voice sound neutral. It doesn't work. Her vocal chords are strangled with jealousy and she wishes she'd just said 'hello' instead.

He smirks at her discomfort and continues to scrub the paint from beneath his fingernails.

'Fine. I'm nearly done. Just the skirting boards and then I'm out of there.'

The work's been taking a frustratingly long time. He finishes a room and then Sarah decides she needs another one painting.

'You must have painted the whole house by now?'

'Nearly, but the outside needs doing when the weather perks up.'

It's a familiar, careworn conversation – Claire tense and suspicious and Steve either dismissive or defensive, depending on how much she tries to push it towards her version of the truth.

She's never seen Sarah but she can't suppress the mental image of her as Bambi, the buxom, sturdy-thighed Bond Girl in *Diamonds are Forever*. He said Sarah had thunder thighs to defuse the situation, Claire knows that, but she can't help but wonder how he knew? Does she wear tight jeans or does she wrap them around his loins while he's grinding his cock into her?

'There, there, my little green-eyed monster,' he grins, as he strokes her cheek with a wet finger.

She lets the matter drop and trudges off to the kitchen to put the kettle on.

Later, when they're snuggled up on the sofa watching television, Steve's mobile phone alerts him to an incoming text message. Claire tries not to invade his privacy and stares at the news presenter on-screen, but he takes so long replying, texting, deleting, retyping, that she looks up in exasperation. She's just in time to see the words 'out for coffee' disappear as the cursor travels backwards again.

'Who was that?' she asks, as he slips his phone back into his pocket.

'Just Mike arranging another job for next week,' he answers, as Claire makes another mental note in her frustrating catalogue of suspicions and anomalies.

In the thick of night, Claire is disturbed from slumber by the trill of Steve's mobile phone. The gloom of the bedroom is illuminated by the blue glow from its screen, but Steve snores on softly beside her.

Claire's heart starts to beat with the thought of the intrusion she's about to make, and the risk of being caught in the act, as she reaches over his sleeping form and lifts the phone from the bedside table. Claire, a bat-blind Mr Magoo without her glasses, squints at the unfamiliar screen. She's resisted getting a smartphone out of inverted snobbery and hasn't a clue how to use it. She swipes the padlock symbol and hunts for the message inbox, accidentally opening up other applications in her ham-fisted incompetence.

'Shit, shit, shit,' she says to herself, wishing she hadn't started this bungling attempt at espionage. She feels sick as she scrolls down the collection of bland text messages about paint colours. What did she expect to find, anyway? Steve's far too savvy to leave sex-texts lying around on his phone.

Then Claire realises with alarm that she can hear the sound of a call in progress. 'Oh fuck! I must have pressed dial.'

She suppresses the urge to throw the phone across the room. Even with the handset held an inch from her nose, she can't make out which button she needs to press to hang up and so she presses all of them. The ones on the front, the ones on the screen, the ones on the side don't do the trick so she shoves it under the duvet and sits on it, while she thinks what to do next.

Steve grunts in his sleep, farts, and rolls over while Claire thinks she's going into cardiac arrest, holding her breath and waiting to see if he wakes up. He doesn't. With the blood pounding in her ears, arse and everywhere else, Claire decides to go to the loo and see what the phone is doing when she gets back.

On her return, she retrieves it from under her pillow to find the screen in darkness. She prays that it has gone back into some sort of sleep mode, but panic rises in her chest as she hears the faint sound of a robot woman saying: 'This is your Orange messaging service, press 1 to listen to your message again, 2 to save your message, or 3 to delete.'

'Oh fuck, I've had it now'. Thunder Thighs must have wondered why he was ringing in the middle of the night, called him back, and left a message on his answer-machine.

She imagines grinding his mobile phone to dust, stamping the evidence out of all existence. Instead, she places it back gently on the table next to Steve and lies there in the darkness wishing the bed would swallow her up. The phone's power light blinks its accusing green eye at her throughout the night.

Supermarket Secrets

'The thing is,' Cindy paused, her nerves tripping her up. 'The thing is, Mr Carter, your Area Manager's boss treats her like shit so she treats you like shit. You feel that your work isn't valued and so you treat all of us like shit. You need to break the cycle.'

Cindy's colleagues sat in the grimy staff kitchen staring at her open-mouthed. This was the most they had ever heard her say, and, even more astounding, she was saying it to their boss, Mr Carter.

'Thanks for that, Karl Marx,' sneered Mr Jones, the Assistant Manager. He shot the boss a knowing look. He hated Cindy for the fact that she had been to university, even if she had been kicked out prematurely.

Mr Carter rolled his eyes and brought the staff meeting to a close.

'Bloody students. Right, you lot – get to work,' he growled.

Cindy's workmates filed out of the room in a reluctant straggle – no one was enthusiastic about starting the day's work. She was left alone in the kitchen with Mr Carter.

'You can clean the fucking toilets for that one, smart arse,' he spat, gesturing to the mop and bucket in the corner.

He paused for a moment, weighing her up with his hard black eyes, and then strode purposefully out of the room.

Cindy didn't mind. At least it was time away from the till and its incessant beeping, not to mention the human flotsam that was constantly washed up in this bargain basement establishment, attracted by its cheap and unwholesome wares. Not a fresh vegetable in sight – just endless rows of two-litre bottles of cola, crisps and sugary breakfast cereals.

When Cindy finished swabbing the toilet floor, she turned the grey stringy mop upside down in its bucket. The ammonia stink caught in the back of her nostrils. She was only using bleach because Mr Carter hated the smell. He might rant at her about it later but she didn't care. She used to be scared of him, but not now. Not after what she'd witnessed at closing time the other night. It gave her the upper hand.

Mr Carter was an aggressive terrier of a man: short, quick and muscular. Cindy found him strangely attractive, but his looks were marred by his red raw shaving rash and the constant film of sweat on his brow. She tried to imagine having sex with him, quick and brutal, she thought.

She had glimpsed that side of him on Wednesday when she'd gone to say goodnight.

Cindy tried to shake off the mental image but it kept resurfacing. The teenaged girl, her face contorted with rage as she threatened him with retribution – her brother from Moss Side and his gun. With Mr Jones holding her still from behind, his beefy arms under her arm pits, her legs had kicked out wildly at Mr Carter.

Cindy walked to her cash register, past the rows of washing powder and through the clear plastic curtains of the walk-in fridge. She eyed the wall of lard with fascination, brick upon brick of solid animal fat. She imagined the huge expanse melting, deliquescing into an oily white sea and sweeping away the customers in its oleaginous wake.

She adjusted her chair and settled herself behind the till. Keying in her passcode, she looked up at her first customer. It was the creepy middle-aged man who kept asking her to marry him. She had changed her route to work since he told her that he watched her walk up Dickenson Road every morning. Now, she was forced to take a longer way, up the back streets, past rows of red brick terraces with their identical net-curtained windows.

Fortunately, it was busy this morning and her stalker couldn't hold up the queue for long. Next, she served an Indian woman, who paid for her bottle of coke with greasy coins retrieved from a carefully folded, empty crisp packet. Cindy stared at the makeshift purse in disbelief, attempting to keep her eyes soft and friendly as she said thank you. There was already enough hatred in this dismal place and, after four months of working there, Cindy could feel it hardening her heart. She tried to fight the ossifying effects of the supermarket, with its cardboard corridors of piled up boxes, but she felt it draining away her compassion with its constant drabness, pointless mind-numbing routine and the unedifying atmosphere of quietly suppressed hostility.

The Asian lady left, to be replaced by a smiling face – in itself a novelty. Cindy smiled back. He was a university student and she'd served him before. She liked his gentle manner. He took his change and said goodbye, pointedly leaving his shopping list on the side of her till. Cindy thought it quaint that he should even have a shopping list – it was usually the old ladies who clutched their precious lists in paper-skinned fingers while they rummaged in their purses for exactly the right money.

The list was written on a strip of lined paper, neatly torn from an A4 pad. She imagined the student writing lecture notes on the remaining pages. It was written in a distinctive curly script; baked beans, eggs, bread ... and a phone number. Cindy's heart pulsed excitedly for a moment, but then she brushed the feeling away as she screwed up the shopping list and tossed it into the bin under her workstation.

The next day was her day off, but when she returned on Monday, she found Mr Carter waiting for her with a smirk on his face. He called her into the Manager's Office. It was a small cubicle with mirrored windows where Cindy often helped cash up at the end of the day.

It seemed that Mr Carter could barely contain himself. 'To the cashier with the brown bob and glasses,' he read with a harsh laugh as he reluctantly handed Cindy the envelope. Cindy recognised the description as herself and she also recognised the handwriting. The edge was torn – Mr Carter had opened it. She burned with anger and pushed the letter deep into the pocket of her overalls. She turned to go, but Mr Carter stopped her.

'Wait, Cindy.'

His face had changed. He was wary again, back to measuring her with his eyes. Cindy knew why and so deliberately relaxed her face, making her voice even.

'Yes, Mr Carter?'

'You never said goodbye on Wednesday. You usually make a habit of it.'

It was true – Cindy saw politeness as a last vestige of her humanity in this brutalising shithole.

'I don't remember,' she replied dismissively, not wanting to give anything away. 'I'd better get on my till – Theresa's out there on her own.'

Later, at the end of her shift, Cindy made her way to the kitchen to collect her bag. She was tired and her head ached from the infernal bleep of the tills. She felt the crinkle of paper in her pocket. The letter had been completely forgotten in the overwhelming monotony of the day. She would read it later. She could guess its contents anyway and wasn't sure they would make much difference to her bleak heart, which seemed to get stonier each day.

She thought back to the young black girl Mr Jones had caught shoplifting – her ripped t-shirt and her bared teeth. Mr Carter and Mr Jones, their brutish red faces twisted with excitement.

'Men – they're fucking animals,' she thought to herself, as she slipped out the back way, past the skips full of cardboard and rubbish, into the drizzle of another grey Manchester evening.

Atomic

Toshiko slipped out of her shoes at the door, placing them neatly with those already stacked there. She felt the familiar sensation of straw matting beneath her feet and savoured the homely aroma of her mother's cooking. Smoothing the skirt of her school uniform, she smiled to herself – Father was home.

Her father, Tsutomu, worked long hours in a drawing office and rarely returned before the children. She felt a pang of concern – perhaps he was sick? She hoped not, as he had promised to continue with his story from the evening before. She had heard it many times, but perhaps Father would remember a new detail today, for her to store away like treasure.

Toshiko greeted her father and seated herself next to him. She regarded the bald crown of his head with a twinge of sadness. Last summer, when she was twelve, her father's hair had started to fall out in handfuls, the thick dark thatch now reduced to a few thin wisps.

'Will you continue, Father?'

Tsutomu inclined his good ear towards his daughter and adjusted his spectacles with a deft movement of his index finger. He was pleased that Toshiko was now hungry for details of his past. For some time he had sensed that she was a little wary of him. This, of course, was due to the swathes of bandages he had always worn. For the first twelve years of her life, Toshiko had never seen him uncovered. Now, thankfully, they were gone.

'Where did I get to, child?'

'At 8.15, the clocks stopped,' Toshiko responded.

'Yes, daughter. One moment the city was all bustle and life – children walking to school, workers riding on the street cars and then . . .'

80

'Pika-don!'
'Indeed, Toshiko – flash-bang!'

On 6th August 1945, Tsutomu Yamaguchi, a draftsman for Mitsubishi, had been visiting Hiroshima on business. That morning, he was due to visit the shipyard, but he realised that he had forgotten something and went back to fetch it. This uncharacteristic act of forgetfulness possibly saved his life. The company's building at the shipyard was devastated by the blast, as 'Little Boy' detonated above the city.

The atomic bomb was released from the American B-29 bomber, Enola Gay, its fall slowed by a parachute. If it had exploded in contact with the ground, the blast would have been absorbed by the earth, but the detonation was deliberately timed to cause maximum destruction.

The buildings of Hiroshima, many constructed from wood and paper, were blown away by the blast, completely flattened by the force. Roof tiles peeled off – the intense heat fusing them together in strange twisted forms. The landscape became a sea of disintegrated and shattered buildings, contorted skeletons of metal, melted and buckled glass and the charred carcasses of trees.

The sky, which had been blue and cloudless, had sealed the city's fate. Had it been overcast that morning, Enola Gay would not have visited Hiroshima. After the intense white flash, the sky turned black and the sun shone blood red. Fires raged like storms for three days. The city was an inferno. Many of those not killed outright were badly burned and scorched. Calling desperately for water, they headed for the river, which became clogged with their livid, bloated corpses.

'What about you, Father? Is that when you were burned?'
'Yes, child. I was burned over my left side, blinded for a while and deaf, too.'

'But you made it home to Nagasaki?' his daughter asked, still amazed.

'Miraculous, I know,' her father replied. 'I returned to Nagasaki the next day and went back to work. I was in the office when the second bomb came on 9th August, telling my supervisor about Hiroshima. He didn't believe me.'

'Then, pika-don!' exclaimed Toshiko.

'Yes. When the bright light flashed, I huddled under a desk.'

In Hiroshima, an estimated 70,000 people were killed in a moment. However, there were many tens of thousands who survived the initial explosion. Some wandered like ghosts, arms outstretched to ease the pain of their burns. They had instinctively placed their hands over their eyes to shield them from the searing white flash. One man said that he saw the bones of his fingers through closed eyelids, as though viewing an x-ray. The consequence of this protective action was skin so badly damaged that it peeled off and hung in shredded tatters from their fingers.

White light, white heat – hotter than the surface of the sun – destroyed all it touched. Investigators from the occupying US Army later found that Hiroshima was littered with 'Atomic Shadows' – the stain-like impressions of human beings who had been vaporised instantly.

These scientists also discovered that it is beneficial to wear white to reflect the visible and infrared light from an A-Bomb. Some survivors had the pattern of the fabric of their kimonos permanently branded onto their skin by thermal radiation, which had penetrated the darker areas of their clothing. The health benefits are minimal, though, in light of the lingering effects of radiation.

*   *   *

'Mother says that she remembers nothing of the aftermath.'

'It is probably too painful for her, Toshiko. There was no help. She had a baby to take care of.'

'She remembers the rain, though, Father. Black rain – slimy and dirty. It coated her skin.'

'Your mother worked hard helping to clear the city. She got soaked many times. She thinks it was the black rain that made her sick.'

'Where were you then, Father?'

'I fled to the mountains. I was very ill with a fever. There was no medicine or dressings for my burns. The explosion did not kill the flies and my wounds were crawling with maggots.'

'. . . and a hen pecked at them!' Toshiko interjected, wrinkling her nose in disgust.

Incredibly, Tsutomu Yamaguchi lived into his nineties, becoming only one of 165 Japanese people to survive the blasts and radiation of both Hiroshima and Nagasaki. He was the only survivor officially recognised by the Japanese government to have lived through both bombs. The survivors, known as 'Hibakusha', were shunned for many years after the war, their suffering ignored by their fellow countrymen.

Tsutomu became a peace campaigner in his later life, seeing it as his duty to share the true effects of atomic weapons with as many people as possible, in the hope that they would never be used again. His daughter, Toshiko, now continues this work.

Breakers

'There's a smokey on my tail!'

'That's a big 10-4, Miss Piggy.'

Clint and his sister were chasing each other on the grass in front of the caravan, speaking into their imaginary radio handsets. The girl was blonde and colt-like with skinny tanned legs; her bright green halter neck top revealed early hints of breasts. Clint was a slightly smaller version of Ruby. You could tell they were siblings; they both had the same scruffy flaxen hair, hesitant smiles and wary brown eyes.

'What's your twenty, Flash Gordon?'

'Behind Uncle Jim's car!'

'10-4, Good Buddy.'

They were having fun together now, but this wasn't often the case. Their father's divide and conquer strategy drove a wedge between them years ago, ensuring that they mostly treated each other with suspicion. With Dad away working, this time by the sea gave welcome respite from his thunderous temper and unpredictable ways.

Clint's cheeks were flushed, his fringe quiffed with sweat. Ruby flopped down in the shady patch of tall grass between the caravans and began to pick the long stalks, tickling her legs with the soft ripe seedheads.

Clint looked at Ruby playing in the grass and lay down next to her, resting his head near her smooth brown shins. He hated her most of the time, but the sun had turned her pinched face pretty, with a scattering of freckles across her nose. Her smile made him feel a pang of something; affection, perhaps. She seemed happier than at home, but she was still moody. This morning, she nearly bit Mum's head off when she asked her to fetch Uncle Jim over for breakfast.

Ruby noticed Clint staring at her. She met his eyes directly and smirked.

'Cock or hen?'

'Hen.'

She ran the blade of grass between her thumb and forefinger so that the seeds bunched up into a green rosette.

'You win!' She tossed the grass grains at Clint's head.

He grabbed her foot, throwing aside her pink flip-flop, and sucked hard on her big toe. She squealed and wriggled in disgust, but this just made him suck harder. Ruby cried out for Clint to stop, squirming in the grass, flinging her free foot around wildly. It made contact with his head, which riled him. He pinned her down and started pummelling her with his fist.

'Clint! Get off her now!'

Clint's mother grabbed him by the back of his t-shirt and pulled him upright. Ruby's face was red and tear-streaked, her clothing stretched out of shape. She looked at the ground and spat blood and froth onto the grass.

'Get your things together, you two – we're going to the beach. Ruby, you can go with Uncle Jim.'

'That's not fair!' shouted the boy. 'She always gets to go in his car. She's out every night talking on his CB Radio – I'm not even allowed to touch it.'

'Just do as you're told. You obviously can't be trusted, so you're coming with me and Gran.'

Clint was sitting at the wobbly table in the caravan with his Gran. His mother stood near the gas hob, waiting for the whistle of the kettle. Clint sighed. He was bored and still felt hot from the beach. His shoulders throbbed with sunburn. Where had his sister got to with Jim? They had left the beach at the same time as them. He idly regarded the flowery curtains, tied back in neat bunches like girls' pigtails.

He jumped to eager attention and looked through the window as he heard Uncle Jim's car pull up outside. Ruby jumped out of the passenger side and strode quickly over to their caravan. She looked unhappy, hunched up, hands buried in the pockets of her sweatshirt. Jim didn't move from the driver's seat. He was probably fiddling with his CB Radio, thought Clint. Jedi Jim, he called himself when he talked to his CB Radio buddies. Clint had listened to their chat, but it was mostly boring, apart from the funny 'handles' and call signs.

'Where did you get that?!'

Clint noticed Ruby remove a Dracula ice lolly from her pocket where she had been hiding it. She started sucking on it and her lips stained blood red. Her face changed from sad to defiant. She looked at Clint, her eyes sparking like flint, daring him to say more.

'Where's mine?'

'I asked Jim to get you a Funny Feet at the garage, but he said it would have melted by the time we got here,' she pouted.

'It's not fair – you're always getting stuff.'

'Enough, Clint,' Mum said firmly. 'Deal the cards out – we'll play Donkey.'

Clint's heart sank, anticipating a night of boredom and humiliation.

'I'm sick of Donkey. I always lose.'

'Eeyore!' mocked Ruby, laughing.

Jim squeezed himself in at the table next to Ruby, so they dealt him in. He was squashing her up against Gran. Ruby shifted uncomfortably in her seat.

Jim noticed Clint's resentful look towards him. 'Sorry, I'll get you a lolly tomorrow,' he said. He looked at Clint from underneath his dark eyebrows, but it was more a threat to keep quiet than an act of conciliation.

Clint bolted out of the caravan and into the twilight. The grass felt cool and damp beneath his bare feet. Laughter and shouts of 'Donkey! Donkey!' rang out through the cardboard-thin caravan walls.

Clint grabbed the stupid homemade paper donkey mask off his head and threw it to the ground, tears of humiliation stinging his eyes. Why did they always gang up on him? Ruby was such a traitor, egging Jim on like that.

'That stupid bastard Jim,' he muttered under his breath.

He walked over to Jim's car and tried the door handle. It opened. He looked at the CB Radio and ran his hand over it. He couldn't harm it – it was Jim's pride and joy. He wasn't even allowed to touch it, only Ruby. Jim would murder Clint if he messed with it.

Looking down at the driver's seat, he saw Jim's caravan key lying there – it must have fallen out of his pocket. Clint imagined scraping the serrated edge along the side of Jim's shiny car, scratching angry words of hatred into the paintwork.

Clint looked around. The curtains of the caravan he and Ruby shared with Gran and Mum were drawn. It shone like a lantern next to Jim's dark, empty one. Using the key that he'd found in Jim's car, he crept into the silent space.

He could tell by Mum's shrill laughter that they had started drinking. Jim would be ages yet, so he dared to put on one of the plastic lights, pulling the cord with a click. He nosed around the kitchen area. Jim always ate with the family, so the fridge stood empty and the cupboards were bare. His shaving gear sat next to the sink. Clint ran the soft bristles of his shaving brush against his bare cheek and then set it back on the draining board.

He scanned the objects on the table: an ashtray, matches, blue biro and a notepad scrawled with strange names. Morning Glory, Widow Maker, Chuck Bronson. They must belong to 'breakers' – Jim's CB Radio friends. He spotted a blurred Polaroid of Ruby and his heart thudded in his chest.

Jim hadn't bothered to make his bed. The white sheets and bedspread were a crumpled, messy heap. Clint spotted something bright peeking out from beneath the covers. It was one of Ruby's colourful sun tops.

Clint retched. Rage welled up inside him. He grabbed the pad and wrote in angry, scrawling capitals.

MISS PIGGY SUCKS COCK.

JEDI JIM DIRTY FUCKER.

He ran out into the night, leaving the caravan door flapping on its hinges.

Mother's Milk

Mother's milk, bitter as dandelion sap,
clabbers my guts to curds and whey.
Drops of spite, expressed with pursed lips;
her venom lactated with acid tongue, until I split.

No gold top for my milksop brother either.
He's no Hermes made immortal at Juno's milky breast.
She's no goddess spurting galaxies and lilies
from teats lactescent.

He's a mummy's boy, slightly spoilt, weaned
on cold tea in his bottle.

I'm no nursling cherub, but bone dry empty
suckler, sickly and ill-favoured.

Just her children; ravenous for love,
raised on Jif lemon and malt vinegar.

Maggy van Eijk

Maggy van Eijk is originally from The Netherlands and now resides in London as a writer and photographer.

In 2007 she won the BBC Young Writer of the Year Award for: "Help, I'm Trapped in a B-film".

Her poetry, jam-packed with images of alienation, broken families and failed relationships, has previously appeared in Ariadne's Thread, Carillon Magazine, Inside Out, ABCtales, ArtFist and Etcetera.

Cowgirls in Oxford Circus

This is the part where a Dutch girl
loses herself in smoke only
to find herself again in the
letterbox eyes of an Iranian
woman at the back of a bus
heading two stops away from
where she really ought to be

This is the part where a librarian
with a pierced nose and fifty percent
shaved head chases a rude boy down the
poetry aisle after he slobbers
milkshake all over Ginsberg's
Cosmopolitan Greetings
he forgets to note its location
as he runs runs runs to

The part where a Portuguese filmmaker
pretends he's asking for directions
and slides a phone number into the
Dutch girl's pocket as she tries to
emphasise she's new here and she
has no idea where she's going

This is the part where a Chelsea
local vomits her muffin into
a Starbucks loo whilst her friend scoops
whipped cream like she's
shovelling yellow snow

This is the part where trench coat men
with funnelled eyes plot and plan their

way through the Gherkin like worms in
and out of rotting fruit

And this is the part where teenagers
from Texas rodeo their way
through Top Shop past smart trousered women
with clipboards who tally up wide
eyes and stuck out hipbones.

These are parts
that spin so fast
and do not stop unless you catch them
with a piece of paper and a
ballpoint pen and even then

they might disappear, like that man you saw
crying on a Camden bridge.

Driving to Whitstable with my father

When people look into our car, they see me
a hitchhiker of twenty-three passenger seat, hands on knees
eyes fixed on a hole in my jeans.
I am too busy to speak
too busy making apologies
for everything
that's going to happen.

I'm sorry I won't make you laugh as much as your friend
the ski instructor with the whippy blonde hair.
I'm sorry I won't be like that woman who comes round
white boots and hiccups
licking her wine
as she mews across your kitchen floor.

How much more
of our
stereoscopic
lives
can we blend and stitch?

Because neither of us knows
how to tell the truth.

I remember porte de bras
in front of other people's parents
secretly imagining them
as a sea of affection.

I remember
cutting my toenails so short they bled
and removing plasters in slow and painful ways,

and that time Mum drove off for days
because the sight of us made her mad
and you chose Italian landscapes and ashy shades of blonde.

You were the first to break my heart
the primal wound, the blueprint for all others.
In my writing
someone like you
is always leaving.
I wish I could make us something beautiful, a forest
with Charles Aznavour singing For Me, Formidable
and we could dance, my feet on top of your feet
sweeping through the trees
you are the one, for me, for me, our never-ending story but . . .

I'm sorry I can't tell you how to be my parent
I'm sorry about your monoglot affection
I still can't decide if it's your fault or mine
blame dances around my head
like a postcard with
an illegible address.

I blink and shrink the houses along the road
and you clear your throat
to tell me something

about lobsters
or something.

Diary of a daughter that didn't get the part

1.

You lie miles apart in sleep as I cling
onto consciousness in my camouflage
of static black, thick like tar, thick like shame
in a house of mirrors I can't escape.

There's a haunting here

taking shape beneath the sticky smell of
your tulip breath – in and out – connecting
me to you

as I lip sync the words
that were never exhaled.

2.

On Sundays we performed with cherry pie,
sometimes for the man with the walrus
moustache. I practiced silence until you
summoned me to play the part of the ditzy
waitress, presenting us on a plastic tray –

he bit my pretty cakes
in two

I fled into the gleam of our chrome plated
kitchen, filling tins with chokecherries, my
back turned away from that pottery mug
held together with tape.

There is a special way of feeling shame,
deep enough to keep silent, that grunt next door
was always too late
as you hauled me through the air, sugar flakes
falling from my lips, me –

unpeeling over kitchen tiles but it's
okay, it's okay, a suture of hope
holding my heart in place.

3.

Huddled in the bathroom – our faces close
almost like love I'd dare myself to think,
straining my eyes so we'd bleed into one
until

a Chinese burn across my skull as you
twisted my plaits like a noose

stop talking about it.

After we watched that hospital show
I noticed how you wear your emotions:
like a stroke.

4.

The worst days were spent alone in my room,
the anemone-glow of a self-inflicted wound
my voice trapped beneath my tongue, a cry
caught in a barbed wire mouth, then suddenly
a shuffle under my door, paper folded tight.

sorry, kid

I swallow it whole, I am nobody I
know, I am fourteen years old and I have
given up, mouse-clicking towards a place where
self-destruction is encouraged.

5.

It is almost day, I leave
before you wake, taking in
the smiles of a holiday in Spain,
smiles that threaten to hook
their glistening teeth onto
my skin. I pull away

dazed beneath the curdling
sky, I plant my feet for the last time

I count my scars and think about
the possibility of us
a constructed coming together
but this seems to be an end
where we split in two
and only just survive.

Imaginary Heartbeats

People nothing but people
on either side of the room and mainly clustered round
speakers in cacophonous flocks.

Dull eyes hide behind shadows and shades and blue-red
glasses of wine as they waste tobacco on false lashes and
promising looks.

Bits of burnt rizla flake and fall
onto the Persian rug and

I retreat into Johnny's kitchen
shovelling dips, counting stacks of cheese.

A shield from boys with peach fuzz chests and girls
with nipples that perk and point through ironed hair.

Who is the self-satisfied blonde? I ask, feigning disgust
his knitwear is only out-woolled by yellow curls
that bounce around his ears and then

he looks at me with chough black eyes
I am funnelled into
his line of sight.

I feel my clothes fall apart around my feet
in nudity we meet, dancing in marsh mellow snow
that we catch between our teeth

but –

he kisses Johnny on the lips
and strokes his thigh, a pewter gleam dots his eye

and I
run outside to strike a match
and exhale

another night.

Leonard

A waning heart drifts
over London's peaks
sleepy concrete that
makes me remember
a boy, crazier than me
and how I shrugged him off
like an ill-fitting blouse.

At three in the morning
in a Turkish café
he turned to me to say:

"my biggest mistake was being born"

I dismissed it
with a kiss just
to stop him from
making more
theatrical statements.

I didn't acknowledge the
depth of his feeling because
I couldn't believe anyone
went deeper than me:
a selfish teenager with skin
made of silk, delicately woven
from inexperience. Not knowing
how bodies can bind together
without minds, without futures
without promises.

The last cab ride to Brighton

he put on a tie and I slid
into my mother's heels
his eyes were alight
like a nightclub on fire
and I was in there, somewhere
and still am
and I'm sorry I left to go home
and I'm sorry he kept on into the night
leaving a trail of smoke and cinders
for some other girl
to pick up
to follow.

The Wanting

Greasy and hung-over on a South Eastern train
I busted out of London's smog-cocoon, where
I had once again reached
the full limit of myself.

I bought instant coffee from a man with eyes
as cloudy as semen. He blinked his ugly DNA
and I blinked back and told him, if he wanted to,
he could have my heart in a bowl
and rip it into confetti,
but he never replied.
Like foldaway furniture
I packed up my hope of companionship.

I walked through Beach Alley, where I realised
there are two types of people; those who think
too much about dying, and those who'd rather die
than think about death.

I only fear death when I'm in love, part of
a diaphanous whole.

I scratched a pebble with a shell and the shell broke.

Existence is beautiful, but it's never whole,
with a fist full of seawater I wiped away
the last of his Atrazine love that trickled down my
thigh from time to time.

Somewhere along the harbour I decided: I'm going to be fine.
My heart may be laced with the gentle deaths of one-night stands but

I'm young enough to laugh it off and I laughed so loud I heaved my liver out onto romance novels in the 95p bookshop.

The wanting is what I fear the most
the wanting.

Blueberry Pie

My dad and I have
blueberry pie on Sunday
afternoons

we meet in the lobby
of Chateau Marmont
and intertwine our
lanky arms to form
a pretzel-shaped hug

we won't get much
closer than that
not in words or touch
or breath and I do admit,
I desire
sometimes
to tell him –

he kisses hello
a needle-thin blonde
who plucks a blueberry from my plate
and my eyes escape the ruinous
site of broken pastry
and stolen fruit but
outside is even less
promising as the
afternoon drizzle
drips down
like a runny nose

and as I do
after every Sunday

I light up, smoke up
and tell myself to
shut up as I patch together
a father of sorts, from these
blueberry afternoons

Things you'd only tell your mother in a foreign language.

It's ten o'clock on a Friday night.
You're pulling hard on my shoulder blades
like you're trying to open me up.
Tiny bones of fear block my throat
and the wind sucks greedily on my hair.

I arch back, to let the worst flood in.

Remember when our feet met
beneath a cubical door?
Shuffling a pregnancy test
in an abandoned receipt.
Back when safe sex meant
swallowing 2 litres of Pepsi
after midnight.

Remember when you held my ponytail?
When too much tequila
forced me out of myself
and I mounted
the streetlight behind our house.
Can you picture it?
The one that made everyone glow like day old piss.

This is my mind, formerly quiescent,
bringing up memories until
my eyes go red. Sometimes I punch
myself in the nose
just to clear my head.

You and I, we fought them all;
loveless adolescents
and deadbeat dads.
We ran
fast
and sometimes
we stopped
not to catch our breath
but to look behind
to see how everyone else
stood frozen by our speed.
I never want to fall asleep
my fingers wrap around your wrist
to feel your pulse
hammering out the proof.

Because life is just a taking away
slow, the way the sun slips out of the sky
and spit trickles down a wall.

I'll settle for being afraid
for being tongue-tied until we untie
until we break.

I just want to be
where you are. Always.

Typing heartbreak into Google

Girl walks into a bar
red dress flares up in the corner of his eye
I-I-I the stammer of a pick-up line.

You wanna be the pathogen?

I'll be the leukocyte.

We were infected, our love spread
like a common cold coughing up
luminous doughnuts we placed
above our heads.
Together we shone brighter than a sex shop
sign that promises everything we already have
but multiplied: girls girl girls open all night
a brightness that blinds, tricked by our own
ectoplasm, a hoax, a smoke screen until
we slipped into silence.

Two days after you broke up with me
I asked Google a question:
Will heartbreak kill me?

Google told me it might.

There's a hole deep down in my throat, it's swallowed my voice
like that space under the seat of your car where everything disappears
oyster cards, theatre tickets, love letters.
Your car –
the one you carried me into, after you
refused to sleep in my bed and I spent the night
running round Brent Cross like a stray dog.

It was midnight and I felt the cracks
in the pavement for traces of love
the same place I once looked for witches and bogeymen.

A year's worth of memories startle the seas
of my abdomen like a school of fish and
I want to vomit, to vomit you. I hate you, I hate you.
But I also hope, maybe for some fortuitous meeting
on the district line, in a bar, on Leicester Square
and I'll dive back into the wet of your kisses
but then I remind myself that this
is just
you
in Photoshop
and us ending is as certain as the death of a star
our compound is unbound, helium and hydrogen
have burnt out leaving dust.

If Neruda is right
and love is a journey
our fuel has run out.

To the girl
in the bar
in the red dress,

Place the mask
over your nose and mouth
and just keep breathing.

Clarissa Angus

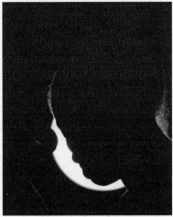

Photo by Joao Santos

Clarissa is a Londoner raised by wonderful Jamaican-born parents.

You can find her online at Ether Books, ABCtales, *The Artillery of Words,* and *Litro* magazine.

Once, she got lucky and made the Bridport Prize Short Story shortlist 2012. Then, she got lucky again and made it into the Raging Aardvark *Twisted Tales 2013* anthology.

Incredibly, her dream of being included as part of the *Liars' League* came true.

She's indebted to anyone who has ever thought her creative musings are worth a read.

Love and App-iness

Ella considers pretending to talk into her phone while secretly taking a picture of the guy who closely resembles the man of her dreams. She'd do it by imitating one of those women who use their mobile phone screens as compact mirrors; touch up her lipstick and eyeliner while taking the picture. Then she'd lower the phone and find him staring at her.

The tube carriage bounces around violently. She abandons the idea for fear of drawing cartoon eyebrows and making an arse of herself.

Screw it! She brings the phone up to her face and purses her lips. She zooms in by enhancing the lens with her fingertips. Up close, he looks clean, though unsmiling; has his head down in a copy of Metro.

Just this one time, she reassures herself, loading the new App-iness app and pressing on 'Take image'.

'How do you not have this app?' Leona asks during their lunch break. 'Everyone has this app.'

Ella chooses to ignore the implication. 'It's invasive. Surely it's illegal.'

Leona laughs.

'Besides,' Ella says, 'people can say what they like about themselves online. It could all be lies, and most likely they are.'

Leona looks thoughtfully at her phone. 'It's a place to start,' she says.

The train is sprinkled with temporary sunlight as the digitised sound of the shutter echoes, filling the carriage.

Her mark looks up.

Taken by surprise, her finger presses down on 'Take image' again. The noise seems louder this time.

The resulting image is absolute. She sees everything, every crevice in his face, the lines surrounding other lines. The frozen look of distaste in hardened plain brown eyes. The frown in perfect HD. Her heart takes a sideswipe at her rib cage. She fights the urge to look up and into his actual eyes.

The app displays its loading screen. It comprises hundreds of strangers' photographs rolling on a continuous loop. None of them look like repeats, but she's never examined them closely enough. Does anyone ever look to see if they spot themselves?

The slideshow fades slightly and App-iness speech clouds float up one by one above it.

Did you know that 67% of App-iness users found their soulmates?

Hint: the first thing you should do after installing the app is upload yourself.

She's never considered taking a picture of herself. Again, her eyes find themselves crawling all over her dream lover. He stares right back.

App-iness was all everyone could talk about. Point your phone at anyone, *anyone*, and learn everything you needed to know about them in seconds. Admittedly she was curious, until Leona tested it on her during their lunch break.

'You won't find much on me,' Ella says, checking the calorie information on her salad before ripping off the plastic lid.

Leona's phone meowed and she watched it, waiting lovingly.

'I deleted my Facebook account over a year ago,' Ella surmises. 'I tried Twitter once. My online persona is as dry as my love life.'

Leona holds up the phone so that she can read it. Beside the information the app gathered is a picture of her, one she thought she'd removed when she deleted her Facebook account.

Name – Ella Roberts, date of birth – 15 October 1980, works in / for / at – civil service, favourite colour – blue, favourite book – too hard to choose, messages sent containing the word 'superfluous' – 23, favourite word derived from messages – 'Love. Pointless . . .'

None of the information is a surprise, but it frustrates her to see the way it's laid out, so black and white – so obvious. So uninteresting.

Leona's smile falters. She puts her phone away. 'There wasn't much more after that.'

Ella stabs at her salad before abandoning it. She eyes the vending machine, gets up and retrieves two packets of crisps. 'What does any of that stuff tell you about anyone? I could have lied about my date of birth. You just happen to know me. And so what? So. What?'

Leona shrugs. 'It's better than nothing, I guess,' she says.

One of the IT guys explained how it worked, like he was pissed off he hadn't thought of something so simple himself. 'It takes a picture and cross-checks it against others of a similar type, against all of the pictures ever uploaded online. It helps if the pictures are tagged, but it doesn't matter if they aren't. Once it collects enough pictures, it stores them on a server, whittling down facial and bodily features until it has a cross section of pictures to eliminate.'

'How the hell does it do that?' Ella asks, while the IT guy pours more wine into her glass. 'All the pictures would be different.'

'Yes. But chances are one picture would have been used more than once,' he says. 'It could have been tagged on Facebook or used for an online CV or job applications. Or,'

114

– he raises two fingers into the air – 'secret government databases. Or pictures uploaded by friends, relatives.'

'What if you're not tagged in any pictures?'

He shrugs, downs his scotch and puts a lazy hand on her knee. 'Then it cross-references all CCTV footage – if it doesn't do that initially. Everyone is on a system. Anything anyone has ever done is on the internet.'

He looks at her meaningfully as the pub lights dim and the makeshift dancefloor fills with Friday night after-work bodies. 'No sense fighting it,' he says.

The photograph that appears on her phone is one of her dream man smiling directly at the camera. Next to it is the section dedicated to supplying the subject's written information, the way Leona presented hers. She almost mistook him for someone else because the smile was so radiant, the face looser. She does a double take and realises it is someone else.

Name – [unavailable], date of birth – [unavailable], works in / for / at – [unavailable], favourite colour – [unavailable], favourite book – [unavailable] . . .

Ella dares to look up and finds him smiling at her.

'Why not just try talking to me?' he asks, his phone in his hand.

Playing

On the tube, my four-year-old cousin soaks up the soft, evocative looks she gets, like a lonely elderly woman.

'Mummy is dark chocolate and daddy is a Milky Bar, so I'm a caramel,' she announces, smiling at me.

I'll play along – why not?

We're forced to stand, her little face pressed up against my thigh. Someone gives up their seat for us. She clambers onto my lap and asks, 'Can I do your make-up now?'

I say, 'Later, honey,' because she'll forget.

I clasp her hand, feeling aggressively maternal as we stroll through a museum. All of the old artefacts and statues scare her. It's the rotting ancient Egyptian jewellery inside an exquisite glass case that she finds most intriguing. She asks me if she can have a necklace like Nef-titty one day. My heart sinks. Hopefully, she won't turn out to be one of those women. Like her mother.

Outside, fading sunlight kisses the London skyline. The stairs are cluttered with tired tourists and schoolkids. I slump down.

She climbs all over me. 'Can I do your make-up now?'

I feign reluctance and am pleasantly surprised when she laughs. Her crayons are the size of premium cigars. She takes up a bright blue one and gently writes over my eyebrows.

Strangers smile at us as she works. They ask me how old my daughter is. She'll soon be five, I say, feeling a flutter of sadness in my chest.

Mr Brown

Gran says: Put dat box down there and move dat one closer to the sofa, right?

She's seventy-eight going on Shirley Bassey. I cast loved-up eyes over the living room of my childhood and do as I'm told.

Mum pulls a battered teddy bear out of a box. Lint parachutes from its body. One of its eyes is missing. She makes a face and chucks it on the sofa.

Gran yells: Don't throw like him like dat!

I question her with my eyes: Him?

Gran waddles to the sofa and collapses into it, picks up the teddy like a surgeon removing a heart from a tray after a failed operation. She strokes his head, arms and stomach.

She says: This is Mr Brown, and smiles at me.

I look at Mr Brown and force a smile back.

Her living room resembles a car boot sale, items dotted about in ordered chaos. Collections of worn records with songs by reggae artists long dead, gifts from friends back home knowing she was homesick. Plates decorated with angels, cherubs, roses. Candlesticks with half-burned candles still wedged inside them. Coasters, tablecloths, a chipped domino set, wine glasses, doilies. They'd all kept her company since Grandad died.

It's the photographs I like best. They're miniature portraits of a time before Mum and I, some of the history recorded in school textbooks. One photograph shows a man with his arm around Gran's twenty-inch waist. Gran's smile is blinding, her skin the colour of holiday brochure sand. The man's face is a beige sun. He stares down the camera as if it's a little too close.

Gran can read minds: Never min' who him is, she says.

The plan is to dump most of what she doesn't need any more and recycle whatever can be saved. By plan, I mean

Mum and I, and her 1990 Ford Fiesta, doing forty-minute trips back and forth to the recycling centre and the local skip.

Gran points to things she wants to consider one last time before their ultimate rejection. Mum and I pass them to her in a human conveyor belt. I'm ordered to put on one of her old LPs, on an actual record player.

I grow bored and restless and decide to take a break. I go to the kitchen, put the kettle on the stove and line the bottom of three mugs with camomile teabags. Sunset threads itself through Gran's yellowed blinds. The kettle rumbles a tiny thunderstorm. I pour the water into the mugs and watch the teabags partially burst open. I see myself at seventy-eight, making tea in a kitchen just like this, with Mr Brown for company. That wouldn't be so bad.

I put the mugs on a tray and make my way out. Mr Brown sits on the kitchen table. Mum wanders in asking if the tea's ready. I ask: What did you leave him there for? She looks to the bear and shrugs.

The softness of the reggae music compliments our unconventional tearoom setting. We sit either side of Gran. She had to leave things and people behind in JA, she tells us, reaching across the sofa to the coffee table for Mr Brown.

At least I got to take him with me, to remember the good times, she sighs.

I don't remember picking him up from the kitchen.

Mum finds a photograph of herself as a girl of eight or nine. It's been altered by cardboard elements, the caramel tone of her skin looking like a watercolour. She sighs like a woman trying to remember something important.

I look again at the man in that photo, who looks right back.

He's the colour of caramel.

Camomile tea always makes me want to pee after one sip. The bathroom is upstairs by the master bedroom. I take the detour. The room smells of peppermint and Oil of Olay. I smile at the enormous trunk I used to hide in at the foot of the bed, aged three. At the bed I used to jump on, its mattress now visibly sagging. Through the window that faces the park I'd run away to, pretending I had things to think about, even now.

Gran still has that picture of Grandad in a frame on the bedside table. He doesn't stare the camera down. He's turning away as the camera captures most of his back, his deep, dark ebony face at a shy, modest angle.

I clock a cardboard box tucked into a corner beside the wardrobe. Maybe there's better tat inside. Gold-plated trays, or jewellery, or anything I can convince Gran to let me keep or sell, instead of dumping.

I listen out on the landing for voices and hear them both in the kitchen, complaining about my weak tea.

I return to the box. Mr Brown is sitting on top of it.

Somehow, I stifle a scream. To compensate, my heart kicks my ribs.

He plays it cool, stares me down with his one eye. I wait for a second, anticipating the spring he'll make, razor-sharp claws unsheathing from his cotton paws.

My need to pee intensifies so I dash to the loo and lock the door. A quick look in the mirror confirms my thoughts. My eyes say: This is stupid, weird, and impossible. My lips tremble: Girl, you saw him. I wash my hands, dry them until they're raw.

Someone says: That man in the photo could be an old friend. Mr Brown is sitting on the floor by the bathroom door. My heart roundhouses my lungs. He doesn't move.

Shaking, I hesitate before picking him up. I'm not instantly scalded. I don't smell sulphur. Fear makes me clamp my fingers tightly around his throat.

Mr Brown says: Open the box. His lips don't move.

I return cautiously to the bedroom and open the box. I find more wine glasses, candlesticks, faded and worn paperbacks. A leather diary.

Possessed, I scan the tattered pages, Gran's handwriting looping at the parts she must have found hard to write, but did; true Iron Gran. There are a lot of those parts.

I have one eye on the bear and the other on the pages. My ears are satellites roving for movement on the stairs.

A small passport picture of that man falls out, with a crumpled dirty note: "The chil' is yours. Come soon, baby."

I look at Grandad's picture. His back tells me he knew.

I look to Mr Brown with bile rising in my throat. He's nowhere to be seen.

I realise I'm crying only when water drips onto my hands. This is ridiculous. I think this on repeat as my gut sinks to the floor, knowing that everything about this house has changed. I close the box and make my way to the bed, lying down on Grandad's side.

Mum pokes her head in: You alright, babes?

I wipe my eyes and tell her I feel sick, that I'll be down in a second.

She says: We're going in a minute. Your grandmother's tired.

As she returns downstairs I feel my heart chase butterflies.

Mr Brown is beside me. His head nudges my hand.

I sprint to the toilet and throw up.

Gran sees Mr Brown in my hands as I walk into the living room. Suddenly the music sounds dated and loud. The scent of camomile is cloying, making me want to retch. The living room is full of old, useless, pointless crap. A demolition site. A fucking mess.

Gran says: What tek you so long?

I love her. I pity her. I might actually loathe her.

I say: I saw another box in your bedroom. Should I get it?

She pauses before speaking; a first. Not today, she says.

I hand her Mr Brown. She takes him with one hand, the other holding that picture.

In the car, Mum worries about her mother. She talks about having her stay with us, at weekends or something. I say: That's a good idea. I don't say: I'm never going back to that house.

I sink into the car seat, let the motion of the car calm me. I'm four again in Grandad's arms as he gently rocks me.

Mr Brown sits on the floor by my feet.

Decisions

In the café, I find an empty booth, slot the last of my change into the oxygen metre and take a seat as the glass door slides shut behind me.

I remove my oxygen kit and place it carefully in the empty chair to my left. I tap my order into the tablet embedded in the table; reconsider, and add a double chocolate chip muffin to go with my latte. I make my music choice: slow jazz. I adjust the temperature, turn the heating up a little. I needn't worry about the expense – Kane will take care of it when he gets here. I give the digital timer a quick, unnecessary glance. There's still fifty-nine minutes of oxygen left in the tank.

My skinny latte and muffin arrive as Kane does. The barista takes his order while hurrying him into the booth. An order taken by a person – it's a rarity nowadays.

Kane orders a raspberry tea. He takes off his oxygen kit and gives me a knowing look before sitting down, like he's read my mind and discarded it on a seat on the tube. He takes off the trench coat I bought him a long time ago, which he keeps at his office – throws it casually over the back of the chair opposite mine. 'So, how much do you need, Lorna?'

I think about it – how much is really enough? To pay the rent and a few bills? To get my hair done using one of those 'chemical-free Afro enhancers'? To drink myself into alcoholic oblivion until Monday morning?

'Only enough to see me through until the end of the month,' I tell him. It's the most difficult answer I can come up with because it leaves him very little room to ask me questions. Only two or three, max.

The barista reappears at the window of our booth and points to the button next to the tablet – the intercom. 'Your tea is on the way, sir,' the barista reassures. The speaker makes him sound out of breath. 'Would you like anything else?' he asks.

'Yeah – get me an espresso, too, will you?' Kane says.

I take the tip of my finger off the intercom and let it hang in the air long enough for its new red coat to glint.

As he leaves, the barista knocks his head against the side of the window. Panicked, he double-checks his oxygen kit before moving on to the next table.

'How do you keep getting yourself into this situation?' Kane asks me. Question one.

I stir my coffee and take a sip. I pick up my muffin and look at it the way you know it will bother someone watching and waiting for you to eat the damn thing. I put it down without taking a bite. I play a scale on an invisible piano with one hand. Every second wasted is a countdown to the lie that will inevitably fall from my mouth and spill all over the table.

Kane's hands lie still and symmetrical, a coffee cup distance apart. His lips are set to serious. He's trying his hardest not to raise one eyebrow. I stare at them. His eyes slip briefly to my chest. He'd be irresistible if he wasn't so married.

The best reply is nothing.

Immediately, he shakes his head from side to side. 'Nah, you're going to have to do better than that.'

Someone drops their mug – it falls to the floor and we hear it shatter into pieces, porcelain lightning and thunder. We turn to see an old man alone inside a booth just across the way from ours. We see everything – he grabs his own throat and coughs, makes strangled, strained noises, falls to the floor in a heap. The digital timer located on the outside of his booth flashes bright green: last warning. He would have been alerted to the one minute of oxygen remaining before he hit the ground.

I can't take my eyes off him. Baristas in matching purple outfits flood outside his booth, stand by his door, watching, shouting orders at one another. The sliding door opens and closes by a hairline – he's managed to build a blockade that obstructs the door from the inside.

'Holy shit,' Kane says.

I grab his hand and he squeezes it.

The man beats one hand on the floor, struggles to raise his head up to look at the rest of us. His eyes catch mine before they scan, bloodshot, to a couple sitting in another booth across the way. He points at them and they freeze with a familiar guilt. The baristas have formed a human battering ram and pound at the door again and again, pointlessly, with everything they have.

The old man passes out.

Kane's on his feet. He looks at the old man and then at me. He sits down again, slowly.

One of the baristas decides the cost of broken glass can come out of his pay. He lobs a chair once, twice, five more times at the door, finally producing crystal, metallic rain.

The others make it inside and one clasps a mask over the old man's face while another holds up an old-school oxygen tank, not an oxygen meter. When was the last time anyone saw one of those? They have to negotiate a mess of beard before they secure it over his nose and mouth. Breathe, they tell him. Just breathe. They all wear their own oxygen kits. We wait a painful, quiet minute. The old man doesn't move.

'Stop looking,' I tell Kane, my eyes never moving. 'You'll only make it worse.'

Our barista returns, and the door slides open and closes at super speed. He brandishes another helping of drinks we didn't ask for, and two colossal croissants. He stands dead centre between us and the scene behind him.

'Would you like anything else?' he asks.

'No, thanks,' I say.

'Jam? Butter?'

'No. Thanks,' Kane says.

The barista moves, and the old man, everyone, is gone.

We drink in silence. The other question he wanted to ask me is now a frown on his forehead. Soon, he'll remember it. In a minute, while we take our pre-paid breaths and calm down.

Outside, the sky is about to rain fire. Sunset bleeds into the backdrop of Oxford Street. People walk past our window, some wearing the latest oxygen kits. They look like wasps without antennae.

'Do you want to end up like that old man?' he asks, taking an exaggerated bite of a croissant.

A gentle hum percolates the air. The second counter embedded into our table lights up – thirty minutes remain.

'Yes. I want to end up choking on my throat like that old man.' I drain my coffee and demolish the croissant. 'Because I can't live without you. Obviously.'

He studies the table as if looking down into the other side of the world. 'After this, I won't be lending you any more money.'

I've not paid him anything back yet. Not one bit-coin. 'OK,' I say.

He was kind enough to buy me the oxygen kit for my birthday. It has a hair-sized fissure close to the top of my right eye, but it's nothing to worry about. Until it is. He wears the latest model. His wife bought it for him.

'I'll transfer the funds tomorrow,' he says.

I say thank you, wondering how long I can live like this. Perhaps until he's truly bored of me.

We get up to leave. He pulls me close and kisses me the way he did when he first believed I was a welcome, necessary distraction. Then he kisses me again and for the first time I'm worried he might mean what he says about the money.

Outside, I put on my kit and make my way to the tube station before changing my mind and grabbing a bus to save money.

The thick air clings to the windows. A whisper of this stuff will kill you in a heartbeat, the news apps say. My heart beats, hard. It does every time I'm on my way home and expect to see my oxygen meter reading: low.

I imagine my death will be a peaceful one, when I'm asleep and dreaming of the time before Kane, when I knew about other things. I'm not yet sure that I'm ready to decide between life and death.

Big Girl

The boys stare up at the scaffolding and make plans about how to climb it. I watch Otis as he talks. He's the tallest and the best looking. He's fifteen and I'm ten, but one day, I'd like to marry him.

My cousin shushes everyone, looking at me. He says: Go home, Kyla. I stick my tongue out at him and tell him I'll rat him out if he tries to send me away.

Otis spots a plank of wood and places it against a railing. It'll work as a ladder without rungs to reach the first level of the scaffolding. The rest is an uphill maze for anyone who's as badass as Spiderman. He asks: Who's going first?

My cousin says Otis should go first. The others ask why. It's decided my cousin will be first, seeing as it's his idea. They don't notice that I'm not beside them until I've reached the very top.

From up here, I can see the edge of the world – a thin, pink line. I can't see how I'm going to get down again without jumping for it.

I think: They laugh, but those girls in my class can't do this.

I jump. As I fall, I hear the boys' shouts rise. I feel macho, and petrified.

I land on my feet. The impact shoots hot white pain into my calves and ankles. I topple and land on my chin.

My cousin panics: Are you stupid or something?!

Otis doesn't say anything. He picks me up and carries me home. He smells like cotton.

Claudine Lazar

Claudine was born in Nigeria, grew up in London, currently living in Suffolk next to a field (which can get a bit windy sometimes).

She tries to see the colour in things, even when life is quite black, and to write about them in a way, hopefully, that other people will enjoy reading.

In the end, though, she writes for herself because she's not sure she would want to live in a world where she couldn't.

A Game to Play

Here's a good game for when your partner has flu. It will cheer her up no end, I promise!

It's called 'helping'. If you are unfamiliar with the expression, try breaking it up into two syllables – it will eventually become easier to say.

The Preparatory Moves:
These can be repeated over the course of several years
- Make sure you have no idea how any of the following operate; the dishwasher, the washing machine, the tumble drier, the cooker.
- Pay attention to the following skills, which you will also need to avoid acquiring; ironing, cleaning, sorting out a trip switch on a fuse board.

Cooking:
Cooking knowledge is OK, so long as it was gained on one-day courses you have taken during holidays to exotic long-haul destinations. Feel free to offer useful advice when someone else is cooking – ie. 'Are you sure that's the proper way to cook rice? The monks always washed it three times in spring water when they showed us.'

If ever asked to actually cook, make sure you fuck it up really badly.

You may still buy useless gadgets and implements. The larger the better, but don't open the boxes.

Microwave skills are permitted.

Shopping:
When asked to visit a supermarket and given a list, make sure that you substitute at least 30% of the items for different ones. If questioned, say, 'they didn't have it', in a confident

tone. Never say, 'I couldn't find it'. It doesn't sound like you tried. Following these simple instructions, it is highly unlikely that you'll be asked to do it again.

Other useful tips for around the house:
Practise not noticing things – the paper you dropped, the tea you spilt, that light bulb that needs changing. This is probably best achieved if you only look straight ahead.

Curtains don't need to be opened or shut. Leave them as they are.

Never lock an exterior door.

Wear noise-cancelling headphones to shut out the annoying ring of the doorbell or telephone.

Never put the loo-seat down. No one will really notice if you miss.

On Sundays, especially, see how many exciting and unexpected places you can leave different sections of the newspapers. Think of it as a treasure hunt in the making. You could have fun with this one!

Ensure your mobile phone is never charged. If someone has charged it for you, leave it unlocked, in your trouser pocket, so it dials a random number. Ignore any odd noises from your pocket until the battery has safely run down again. Put it in a drawer, out of harm's way.

Now go to the mirror. Practise the following – look first eager and expectant – say, 'let me help – what can I do?' Smile winningly. Wait ten seconds. Allow smile to fade. Look saddened. Recoil slightly. Lift eyebrows in a puzzled but uncontentious way (you don't want to start an argument). Shrug. Say, 'well, if you're sure . . .'

When satisfied with authenticity, repeat in front of partner.

Leave room swiftly, with a nonchalant, uncomprehending expression until safely out of sight.

Ten Things As You Drown

1964 and I am actually drowning, in the Thames. I've stopped panicking. It doesn't matter any more that my long hair's made my head too heavy to lift out of the water. Instead, I relax and open my eyes – they were shut tight with fear before – looking calmly around at the green brown golden world. It's so beautiful I don't mind at all. Suddenly it's all spoiled. Hands grab me, pulling me roughly out onto the bank. I feel assaulted by the overpowering light and noise and I burst into tears of anger.

1970. In the garden of an old rectory in Suffolk, escaping from a boring lunch. I'm hiding in a small wood, sitting by a stream on my own, dangling my bare feet in the shallow water. It's deliciously cool and I watch it ripple, tumbling over little stones all shiny wet, polished smooth as anything. Quick as a flash, a kingfisher goes streaking past. I am about ten and it's the most magical thing that's ever happened to me. I instantly decide I am going to have my own old rectory, kingfisher and stream when I am older.

1976. London, in a dressing room with another girl. We've just come offstage and we're laughing and bouncing around the room, stopping every now and again, trying to work out which one of us is still shaking the most. There's a knock on the door and a man hands us our payment for the evening – a bottle of whisky. We're so excited we drink it between us very quickly – it's funny, it doesn't make us as drunk as you would expect it to – and then we head off to a party, still with our white painted faces and heavy black rings around our eyes.

1977. I am stumbling, blind drunk around Paris, with my best friend. It's the first time either of us has been abroad without any adult supervision and we haven't been sober or stopped laughing since we stepped off the boat train. We have our arms around each other because otherwise we would fall in the gutter and we are just totally happy in each other's company. Everything smells a bit off, especially on the metro, but that only makes us laugh more.

1982. Walking along the Promenade des Anglais with my boyfriend. It feels like there is a cushion of air between the pavement and me. We are sharing a Walkman and listening to the Stranglers at top volume as we walk. The evening has just begun to cool things down a little bit but my skin is still hot from a day on the beach. We weave in and out of families and roller skaters, watching the sea to our right as we head to the bar in the Vieille Ville to do our set. People stare at us because we're all in black with spiked-up hair and we look at one another and smile.

1986. In the cellars of a big stone house in Yorkshire getting the rooms ready for a party. I am pregnant and my best friend has cancer. On her neck, as if someone has tried to guillotine her, there is a livid red ring of scar all the way around, from when they tried to remove the lump. We're lying on the damp floor and striking poses against the cobwebbed walls, spray-painting Day-Glo outlines around each other's bodies to decorate the rooms. My best friend's mother comes down and says, 'you're both as mad as each other'. We laugh and carry on spraying.

1992. On a hospital bed while all the doctors and nurses are panicking because my baby's heart isn't beating properly and I need to have an emergency caesarean. He isn't supposed to be born for another two months. Then someone notices I've painted my toenails fluorescent orange to cheer myself up. Everything stops while they wonder where they might find some nail varnish remover and cotton wool. Suddenly the surgeon says, 'we haven't got time for this', and they all start moving quickly again, and I'm wheeled off, terrified, watching the lights on the ceilings as we move along endless corridors, down to the operating theatre.

1996. Two little blond boys come pelting into the kitchen from the garden and they fling several muddy things onto the table. They are so breathless with excitement they can hardly speak. 'Dinosaur bones!' they say. I look at what they've put the table, then at their faces; eyes shining with pride and expectation. I can't bear to let them down, so I say, 'yes, I think you might just be right.'

September 2000. Sitting on a fire escape outside an apartment block in Boston, feeling sad. We all came out to watch a racoon rooting around near the dustbins, and then the others went back in and I stayed on. I'm forty in a few weeks and I'm not sure what I'm going to do with the rest of my life. I turn to watch them all through the window, laughing and talking. There's nothing to stop me going back in – they are all lovely, but I don't want to. I light another cigarette, and wonder what to do next. I feel very alone.

August 2009. I am stepping off a plane and the heat is unbelievable. I am so excited I can't stop smiling. I think something wonderful might be about to happen but I'm not quite sure if it's going to work, and so I'm half-terrified, too. I'm definitely doing the right thing now. In fact, I'm kicking myself for not doing it before. I start walking up the long corridor to the exit.

Madagascar

So sweet of you to lend me this bikini . . . it was a nightmare because they lost all our luggage in Paris . . . yup . . . every single bag except our carry ons. Good thing I put my jewellery in that one. Actually, Mark was a little taken aback when he saw I'd brought this ring.

Yes, it's pretty . . . thanks . . . bit show off, though, isn't it. Of course I wouldn't have bought anything this big – who could afford that nowadays? No, it's a family piece. Yes . . . real! I know, I read that part, too. They do seem rather poor, don't they? But you don't actually have to go out of the airport when you transfer to the little private plane . . . and then of course – here – it's all very different, isn't it.

Oh, absolutely – I love to see the real country, too, when we go away. I mean sometimes you can't . . . I was in Dubai with a few girlfriends last month – oh yes, it was wonderful – the shopping was to die for – but you can't really leave your hotel there – there's nowhere to go for starters. You don't need to anyway – it's all there for you. I mean, what do people go there for apart from the sun and the pool, anyway?

Yup, they do the trip on a Wednesday to the local village. Are you coming, too? Oh good! We can meet up, love to! Your children going? I'm not sure about mine. Freya's sulking. No idea why. Maybe the cases? She's refusing to leave her room – yes, I know, two days and all she's done is watch DVDs. I had to bribe Felix to come out . . . yes, he's nine. I said fifty pounds if he can find five different kinds of lemur to photograph. Children are hilarious, aren't they?

Um . . . no, I don't work – I'm so busy, there never seems to be enough time for a job – I would definitely love to, otherwise. I have my charities, of course. I flew to India a couple of months ago to look at conditions – oh yes, it was fascinating . . . wonderful hotel – marvellous spa, too, and I could keep up with my yoga – India's wonderful for yoga. Oh yes, very poor, but we have these ladies who make things, all fair trade, you know, and then I put them in my auctions. I do love auctions. A lot of work, though, all the organising, and it costs so much – catering, flowers and so on . . . still, it's all in a good cause.

Yes, I generally seem to get away once a month . . . let me see . . . so far this year, Dubai in January, here for half-term, and then skiing next month . . . I suppose it is rather a lot, but one does need a break from London and Mark is just snowed under. Hedge fund management. Yes, they do say that, but he's busier than ever – hardly see him these days. Funny, isn't it? Good thing, though . . . Bedales for three costs a bloody fortune – oh, absolutely absolutely worth it – the ethos, so wonderful. No, the two eldest don't like boarding but it is heaven there, and I'm so busy! Anyway, we can have quality time on holiday. They are the limit, aren't they. That's why Freya's sulking. Says she wants to be at home with her friends. Oh, I'm sure she'll snap out of it soon.

Mark? I'm not sure where he is, actually. Haven't seen him to talk to since last night. Yes, I think he might have gone for a long walk or something. He wasn't there when I woke up. I didn't say anything last night, did I? No . . . not too much to drink . . . well, maybe a little . . . oh God, I'm sorry. Poor you. I didn't, did I? How awful.

What is it, Felix? Oh darling, let me see . . . that's splendid . . . the best ever . . . not until you have five different ones, darling. Well, go and find your sisters, then . . . go on . . . tell them they have to . . . off you go.

Anyway . . . God, I'm so sorry . . . what must you think of me? Oh, no harm done, then. Maybe that's why Mark went out so early. Did you see him? Oh Lord, was he? No, honestly, it's just that when I drink anything it mixes with my anti-psychotics. Oh yes, you should see me without them. With the barman? God, I didn't, did I? Are you sure?

Oh, look ... the manager's coming over. I love those sarongs they wear, don't you? So ethnic!

A note for me? Thank you. Shall we order some drinks now he's here? What would you like?

Goldilocks

Once upon a time, not so long ago, Goldilocks went for a walk in the woods, but no sooner had she got there than she realised she was wearing six-inch heels.

'Fuck that for a game of soldiers,' she said, under her breath, as there were rather a lot of children around, this being a fairy tale and all that. 'I'd sit down somewhere to enjoy the forest ambience but I don't want to scuff my Louboutins.

So she looked around, and lo and behold, there was a little gingerbread-type house thing in a small clearing. Not *the* gingerbread house, because that's a different story, but definitely something very close. It certainly had gingham curtains and sweets round the window frames.

The door was ajar, as all cottage doors seem to be in these places, and so Golidlocks, thinking it might be some kind of themed refreshment solution, decided to go in.

It was quite dark inside – they'd rather overdone the ambient lighting, and it took a minute or two for her to work out that there was no barista, and in fact no counter at all, and not even any menus at the table. However, blisters had begun to form on her feet and, even without the prospect of a caramel skinny latte, she knew she had to sit down.

There were three chairs – mismatched, which she felt added to the boho charm.

Which to try first, though? The biggest, a huge squashy leather Eames chair, seemed the obvious place to start. She teetered over and lowered herself in. Five seconds later – disaster! Her spandex biker leggings had no traction whatsoever on such a smooth surface, and she slid right back off again.

She was determined to keep her temper, so she counted to five, slowly, and approached the middle-sized chair with renewed optimism. It was a rather exciting looking sixties wicker number, very Andy Warhol, so she looked forward to taking the weight off her stilettos. What she didn't realise, until too late, was that original sixties wicker is always going to be uncomfortable, and being a fashionable size zero, she had no padding to take the edge off it. Puzzled and slightly sad that she wouldn't be able to recreate her favourite Edie Sedgwick pose, there was nothing left but for her to try the smallest chair; one of those little inflatable ones. Really quite desperate now, she sank gratefully into its softness. Ah, perfect! And it really was, until one of the studs on her lamb-skin aviator jacket – so this season – punctured the flimsy plastic, and she and the chair ended up on the floor, both quite deflated.

Goldilocks was having trouble finding her inner calm by now and, as so often happened when she was stressed, she began to feel hungry. Instinctively, she reached in her pocket for her iPhone so she could talk it through with her therapist (eating was one of her issues) but sadly it seemed that there was no signal in the forest. That was almost the last straw for Goldilocks, and she looked around wildly for something reas-suring – an egg white omelette, for instance, or even a power shake. She was not an unreasonably fussy kind of person, after all, but the only things she could see were three bowls of what appeared to be porridge.

Everyone has a breaking point, and that was Golidlocks'. She began screaming quite hysterically about how unneces-sarily cruel it was not to offer a carb-free option, completely forgetting in her distress that this wasn't actually a restaurant of any kind. Removing her shoes and putting them carefully in her bag, she ran as fast as she could, not stopping until she had enough signal-strength to call a cab.

So she quite missed out on the beds upstairs, which was lucky because the bears in this particular story had many allergies and could only go out when it was totally dark. This meant that they spent their days tucked up, sound asleep, and they would surely have had quite a lot to say if Goldilocks had started jumping in beside them. They were so not into girls.

What happened, in fact, was that they slept through the whole thing and didn't say much at all when they finally did wake up, thus depriving you of the whole tedious, repetitious ending, which is just as well really, I suppose.

Anyway, despite not having a proper conclusion, I'm sure you'll be thrilled and reassured to know that they all lived happily ever after.

The End.

Las Vegas

'So what would happen if we didn't give it back? If we just kept going?'

It was a throwaway comment – a joke. She didn't really expect an answer. For a minute or two, he was silent; she looked ahead and realised they'd broken free of suburbia. They were suddenly back on the open road, nothing but desert, with only the mountains in the distance to break the dusty brown monotony. Then he said;

'Seventy two hours. After that, they call the police. I already looked it up.'

He glanced across at her for a second, then turned his attention back to the road, but she carried on looking at him. His eyes were the darkest brown you could imagine, and the lashes along the bottom so thick and black, it looked as if he was wearing make-up.

'That would take us to Monday. Pretty much most of Mexico.'

She tried to imagine Monday if they were in Mexico, then how it would be in reality – five hours' dreary layover in New York, en route to Heathrow. They both knew it wasn't going to happen. Suddenly, Sunday, the day she was due to leave seemed like minutes away, and she didn't want to go home.

She moved her arm over towards him, and he took one hand off the steering wheel. Looking at his fingers on hers, she told him she'd never felt quite like this before. He squeezed her hand and said he hadn't, either.

As teenagers in London, they could have done almost anything they put their minds to, and they did do most of it; just not this.

It was a long drive back, and they only stopped once, at a little town called Mammoth, which made her laugh because it was anything but – just a dusty road and a small stopping place, which didn't even sell gas.

Above the door, it said in big letters, 'Everything you ever wanted from Chicago without the 1800 mile drive!' and she tried to imagine what could possibly have brought someone all that way to start a business in such a nothing place. Whatever it was, they must have really believed in that slogan, because it was repeated everywhere – on the napkins, at the till, on the menus, and on the pocket of the white uniform of the smiling man who took their order for sodas and a tuna melt to share.

While they were waiting, she wandered around; half the building was the diner, the other half sold all sorts of odd things – Mexican knick-knacks, musical instruments, fishing tackle. There was also a counter with a notice above it saying, 'Genuine Indian Blankets', and it was true; there were some blankets hanging on wooden poles. They were in lurid, day-glo colours – pink, turquoise, lime green – and they all had a crudely drawn, larger-than-life print of Marilyn Monroe in the middle, her skirt still raised up by that long-ago New York air vent. They didn't look very Navajo to her.

At the Hoover Dam they crossed the state border, which, because it's a sensitive area, had a much bigger, more serious checkpoint than the others they'd seen on their trip.

'Always best not to look too rock and roll going through this one,' he said, doing up one more button on his shirt, 'especially not with what we've got under the wheel arch. For some reason they always go down extra hard if you have a pipe as well – doesn't really make sense, but there you are.'

She sat up straighter in her seat and tried not to think about what could happen if they got stopped, but her mouth felt dry as they moved their way up through the stop-start queue of traffic. A little further on, people in uniform peered into each car as it came to a halt. As they got nearer, a vehicle that had been picked out was parked to one side. It was old and had a mattress tied to the roof with rope, and something in Spanish painted on the side. As they inched forward, a woman could be seen getting out of the passenger seat. She walked slowly to the back of the car where a man was unlocking the boot. Neither of them looked nervous – just very tired, resigned.

She wondered if the woman had children, like she did, and what would happen. Then suddenly it was their turn. She tried to stare straight ahead, but out of the corner of one eye she could see the guard looking them over. He was big and unsmiling, and the sun reflected off the metal of his gun. There was a tiny pause and she held her breath, then he gestured with his hand and they were through.

By the time they reached the outskirts of Tucson, it was five o'clock and they were late. As he reached up to find the remote to open the garage door, she glanced at the temperature gauge, which said 117. It was hot and airless, and when she tried to get out, her legs were stuck to the seat. Unpacking the trunk, they took the bags into the apartment. Once upstairs, he dug out the black from where he'd left it, hidden in a box of vinyl, and gave her the same comic/serious look she remembered from all those years ago. His eyebrows could do things she'd never seen anyone else's ever manage.

'Quick pick-me-up?' and she smiled and nodded.

Minutes later, chasing the little plume of smoke around the foil, the tired hot stickiness lifted and she began to feel better. It had been a couple of days since they'd last had some, in that cheap motel in Ventura where he'd worried constantly about the car parked outside, and the men in dirty white vests leant over the first-floor balcony railings, drinking beer and watching them silently as they'd unlocked the door to their room.

His cellphone beeped, and while he checked it, she suddenly didn't feel so good anymore, so she sat down on the sofa. Glad to be out of the sticky car, she also half-wished they'd kept going forever. Now that they were back, she found it hard to forget about how soon she'd be going home. She pushed the thought away, but then it came back – over and over again, no matter how hard she tried to banish it. The only thing that worked in the end was when she realised she must have overdone things and was going to be very sick at any moment. Who'd have thought you could lose your tolerance so quickly like that, after only a few days?

She was just about to get up and rush off to the bathroom when she heard an odd noise, a kind of croaky squeaking – and a little cat skittered out from under the sofa. She had the face of a Persian, with the flat nose and long hair, but, except for the tip of her tail, the rest of her body had been shaved. It was the most extraordinary thing she'd ever seen.

Looking up, he exclaimed, 'Baby!' and bent down to stroke her. The cat rubbed herself against his hand. Baby was obviously thrilled to see him.

Looking up from the cat, she could see him trying to gauge her reaction:

'Katy must be back. You haven't actually met, have you?'

She tried to say something reassuring, because she knew what it meant and she honestly didn't mind – but as soon as she opened her mouth to say so, she realised she had about ten seconds before she was sick. Running out of the room, she hoped he wouldn't get the wrong end of the stick.

Deborah Hambrook

Deborah Hambrook, artist and musician, lives in Berkshire with her husband, John, and their two rough collies. Interests include music, reading, writing poetry and walking the coastal paths of Britain.

Favourite female poets include Maya Angelou, Sylvia Plath, Wendy Cope and Carol Ann Duffy.

She is currently in the process of compiling a collection of children's art and poetry for publication.

Capturing Beauty

First, I paint on masking fluid,
dragging and flicking to splash needles
where goldfinches nestle amongst the thistles
drawn in faint HB, each waiting
in anticipation of the vibrant
and subtle tints to be applied.

I decide on a No. 2 brush and a No.10,
wet the surface to be worked on,
then blending cobalt blue with burnt sienna,
I shade in a touch of ultramarine.
Next come umber shadows,
and I use chrome yellow and black and white
for the flashy markings of the wings.

For the back-view bird,
I mix the faintest purple, which I blend
with thinned sienna to produce a pale maroon.
To soften hard edges, I wash in extra water
and with dry brush, procure the appearance
of feathers, spotting on
some darker flecks of brown.

Painting on a little yellow
where the red will be applied ensures
the brightest shade. And now
I use a finer brush to bring in sharper detail
before a glaze – transparent wet on dry.

Peeling off the masking fluid,
I wash in the hazy mists of thistles
in pinks and mauves and muted greens.

These form a background where unaware
the finches flock to feed.

No harm that they can't see the net –
so fine, the birds will be deceived;
their freedom soon forgotten –
they'll want for nothing, and I think
they'll be quite happy in a cage.

The Stench of Ignorance

You can smell the homeless,
unwashed and badly dressed –
depressing sights. The druggies
and the layabouts nattering
in gangs, or slouching formless
in doorways, sleeping shamelessly
by day, drunken on steps,
selling magazines –
malingering.

It's hard sometimes, difficult
to avoid their needy gaze;
where to look, pretend
you never saw a face, heard
a request. You do your best
to walk on past without staring,
wishing they weren't there, knowing
they are there by choice –
avoiding jobs – beggars
belief.

Someone ought to round them up
and send them on their way –
anywhere but here, where we are
trying to live a decent life –
make a living, a home, provide for
children – proper people.

Even abroad, you can't enjoy a holiday
without them being there;
their children filthy and hungry.
It makes you sick.

I saw a child of maybe five
lie down in the centre of the street
and go to sleep. I took a photo
to show the folks back home
how the other half live. Shameful!
Something's got to give.

It's one long holiday for those kids –
no school, living off freebies. They'll tell
you that homelessness is loneliness –
that's a lie – there's loads of them –
in towns and parks and streets –
in stations in every town and nation.
You can find them on the net
in glossy photos (getting paid, no doubt)
or captured in artistic black and white.
Posers.

I don't fret about the homeless.
As I've said, there are loads of them,
and only one of me.

Nan

I woke and I knew
that I'd never see her again –

never bathe in her bath
with Imperial Leather and bubbles

eat in her kitchen, or sleep
in my bed at the end of her bed

and hear her tell stories, or listen
to Radio 4, or drink tea

and eat toast and then walk
to the shops at eleven.

I'll never invite her to stay
at my house, and no one will drive

to collect her, the children excited
to have her come stay –

me cooking dinner, and being there at the door
to greet her – all neat in her tweed suit

and smiling. I'll never plonk a new babe in her lap
and take photos of her

thrilled as she was with each one.
I'll never go shopping, or take her to lunch

or hold her small hand as she sleeps
in the hospital bed, kiss her cheek –

say, I love you, I'll see you next week,
and never again

will I hold her, or phone her.
It's been fifteen years since she left

and this morning I missed her –
I woke and my pillow was damp

and my lashes were wet –
from dreaming again that I saw her.

As Autumn Leaves

Studying the veins of drying leaves –
the span of questioning hands,
I note with admiration, nature
painting vivid colours to make beautiful
the process of ageing,

in hope of finding acceptance
of eventual dying, crumbling,
of being scattered to the ends of winds
that disappear beyond the corners of the world.

I find a rare example,
spectacular in swan-song glamour.
Gold, bleeding crimson to damson,
blending brightly pre-decay,
it begs to be remembered; to startle
the world into thinking it was something.

I lay it out with love
and smooth it between two pages of my diary.
Clean sheets, unsullied by comment,
wait where there is nothing left to say or do
but slam the book shut.

Leaves preserving memories,
one day will be found and briefly questioned,
perhaps smiled at, then thoughtlessly replaced
upon a shelf to rot.

I thought I heard the sound of laughter gasp
from between the pages of my life,
but it was just the thought of farewell weeping,
as beauty crushed within.

Crash

In the evening, I witnessed the aftermath
of a crash on a busy road – a woman
sat weeping, surrounded for protection by cars,
stopped to block the traffic.

I went home with her in my head, heard the siren
of an ambulance and felt glad
she wasn't waiting, shocked cold
in the rain and crying, her audience dispersed;
relieved and a little thrilled,
as much as concerned, at a spot of drama.

I went to bed so late that I witnessed the dawn,
dreamt a fitful dream then woke and went to town.

I thought of her
sat at the edge of the road, alone, surrounded –
bought some clothes I didn't absolutely need
and a book I couldn't afford –
and a holdall.

When I got home, I witnessed your face, incredulous
that I had spent the cash we hadn't got to spare on crap
we didn't need
or want, and instead of the apology you expected,
you witnessed me

throwing a finger in the air as I walked out the door,
knowing I'd be gone for good.

Cracked Up

Within the broken mirror
I glimpsed a shattered face, fragmented
in confusion – mosaic madness in the remnants
of a crooked smile.

I handed you the mirror – you looked
and laughed that it was not my face
you saw refracted in it,
but little selves of you – cracked up!

You dropped the glass – we watched
the scattered fragments shiver in the sun
in puzzled paranoia;
the flippant transient pleasure of it
soon forgotten –
how quickly we move on.

Now, when I study mirrors
I see shadows of fatigue.
The polished glass is ruthless, illuminating
blemishes, and in the eyes; belated wisdom
that the only one reflected back is me.

Man

Today, I saw the man
who looks like you – your height,
too-long short hair – almost your double.

But your eyes were blue
and his hair is grey –
as yours might have been by now.

Same determined chin, chiselled
features, you could have been brothers.
He caught my glance and I smiled, unconsciously

remembering the lapping river,
the ripples of sky in your eyes as you flaked
like a star on the grass. He smiled back

and I turned away, embarrassed at being caught
staring. When I checked, he was gone.
I'll see him again and remorse will return

for admiring the smoke you mouthed
and tongued to the clouds' morphing
images, there to amuse us – a drifting dog, a chariot

with horses fading to the beyond, swans
threading by, white feathers,
an angel looking down on us.

I thought smoke rings were important back when
we were immortal and there was only one
like you. If only we had known.

What If

What if you don't know?
What if it's sunny outside,
or you are forced to make small talk
about the weather – mild, grey,
cold, warm? Whatever!

What if you can't check your tears
as you keep your downcast gaze
upon the goods you scan
until it's time to take a payment
and you raise your doll-glass eyes –
apologise as he asks you –
'Why so glum?' It's nothing.

But it *is* something.
It's everything and all of them back home.
Communications cut, the power lines
knitted spaghetti nets of cables
tangled amongst the rubble, the roofs of houses,
sticks and stones, the broken bones of ghosted homes.

In your mind, you're watching people
stepping barefoot through the shrapnel of their lives.
Your mind is wandering through a junkyard city,
past the bloated corpses – unidentified,
just numbers cranking up the death toll
as it rises.

You scan the streets for their dear faces,
praying they were evacuated
to higher ground in time. Praying
they're alive.

But what if last week, you were laughing,
complaining about the weather,
and what if they've been counted?
The customer, impatient – asks you,
'What's the damage?'
You answer without thinking –
'Ten thousand, maybe more'.

Queer As Folk

I saw Salman Rushdie
slurping slushies in a cafe
whilst carefully crunching crackers
seeming knackered and remote

He bit a thickly buttered butty
stiff and oddly dodgy
looking doughy, sick and stodgy
and stuffed it roughly -all disgusting
down his goaty bloated throat

Perhaps it wasn't Rushdie
slurping slushies in the cafe
but some other cranky chappy
getting cross at being stared at
crunching crackers – I don't know

But if it was the sod, it's odd
because although he didn't know me
he got security to throw me
on my arse out of the shop

I couldn't stop them
though I don't know what was wrong
with taking photos of that
strange and creepy slushie slurping
cracker crunching
sandwich munching
weirdy bearded bloke

Goodness me, what can I say?
There's nowt so queer as folk

Rainbow Over Tesco

From the top of the railway bridge,
a rainbow over Tesco
framed a promise –
perhaps an end to the prevailing downpour
and some sunshine –
overdue.

But the vivid colours faded to a dull
unglow, soon erased as heaven darkened
seething back brief joy,

and all the people left the train downheaded
trooping grey across the car park
dodging oily puddles and taking
shelter under pulled up coats, or folded
newspapers. They never saw

the rainbow and didn't feel
the disappointment of a broken promise.
All was as expected

and the sky wept on.

Being Female

I swam and kicked –
flexed my limbs and stretched,

curled my fingers
and fanned my toes,

opened lash-rimmed eyes,
sucked my thumb and slept

fetal, filled a hopeful womb
without a thought of future

plans for school, love and marriage,
motherhood, nor questioned

my potential – dancer, doctor, actor . . .
No fears irked of life's uncertainty,

nor knowledge yet, of loving family –
brothers, cousins, aunts and uncles,

my proud parents, or any sorrow
in the knowledge I will not be born

alive because I am a girl
in a culture that values men

over women – not just there
but here, in Britain.

To Laugh At Terrible Things

I sometimes sat with Steve in his restful room
with the sun streaming in, trimming the edges of his dog,
encircling her in a holy halo, and playing gently
on Steve's features, softening the contours
in a watercolour wash of the face.

I sometimes sat with Steve and laughed at terrible things
that in polite company would have made us feel guilty
for the flippant lack of sensitivity – but laughter is free
and there wasn't much else either of us could afford.

I sometimes sat with Steve and said nothing,
both of us quiet in our lazy lack of get up and go.
Then, too quickly, it was time to leave,
and that is what I did –
I got up to go.

I sometimes sat with Steve, and his dog was pleased
when I stood up to put on my coat.
Then I'd kiss Steve's cheek, and for one whole week
we wouldn't speak, saying nothing at all.

Then he'd open the door and I'd be there again
for a hug and tea, and the dog was displeased,
but she'd know –
I sometimes sat with Steve – then I'd leave,
and she'd be glad to see me go.

Katherine Black

Katherine Black is fifty and lives near Bolton with a screwed-up dog called Charlie and a garden full of squirrels.

One day, when she's grown up, she hopes she will be a proper writer.

She is mainly a writer of psychological thrillers but much of her writing is due to looking for 'Home' in all the wrong places.

Mourning Glory

The raggedy little girl, who was really a beautiful princess but didn't know it, walked into the golden meadow where all the delicate flowers turned their heads to the gilded sun. She called out the name, Glory, twice, and her voice tinkled on the wind like the sweetest bell ever heard.

And so he came.

The magnificent stallion rose to the crest of the hill and trotted, magnificently, into view. He stood for a moment, a black silhouette against the bright, golden sun. Casting his eyes over the meadow that he patrolled as his own, he saw his beloved raggedy princess.

And so he was motion.

His flaxen mane and tail, crimped and flowing, blew behind him in the breeze. The sleek body blurred as he thundered down the meadow, his flight lightning fast while his gentle feet never harmed even a single flower's head; for they were his flowers. A cone of exertion steamed from each of his wide, soft nostrils and his eyes never left the little girl who meant everything in the world to him.

And so he was still.

He nickered as he came to a stop in front of her, bowing his head and easing his velvet nose towards her stubby fingers.

'Oh, Glory, I have missed you.'

The huge white stallion bent down for a moment with the raggedy princess, nuzzling her with all the gentleness of a kitten. She stood on tiptoe to run her hand down his warm, damp neck, his silken mane cascading over to tickle the back of her fingers as Glory touched his lips to the little girl's leg. She giggled as the sticking-out hairs stroked her kneecap and she let her face rest gently against his withers, listening to the great lungs as they drew in and out.

And so they were loved.

The raggedy princess grabbed a handful of mane that was as soft as spun wool.

'Ready, boy?' she asked, and then she vaulted, light as confetti and as graceful as a ballerina, onto the stallion's back. She leaned forward and hugged the gentle beast around his pure white neck. He pawed the ground, anxious to be off, flying towards whichever adventure awaited them. The raggedy princess was the best rider in the kingdom. Her hands tingled as she grasped the horse's mane. She was ready. He was ready.

And so they were ready.

She twitched her calf muscle almost imperceptibly into the horse's flank but it was the only aid that Glory needed to be given. Adjusting her seat, she moved further onto her pubic bone, lengthened her leg, dropped her heel, and became one with him. Child and horse merged into the scenery of the enchanted kingdom as they outran the wind, just for the pure joy of flight.

Shortly, they came to the King's Castle.

'Oh no, Glory, the castle is on fire. Whatever are we to do?'

They charged across the lowered drawbridge, a guard of honour in crackling flames overhead. Paying no heed to danger—for together they were invincible—they set about saving people's lives. One by one, the raggedy princess lifted the occupants to safety. Again and again, they thundered over the blazing drawbridge carrying people safely away on Glory's broad back.

The Crown Prince was so grateful to the beautiful raggedy princess that, at first, he didn't notice her stunning beauty. When he did, he fell instantly in love with her. He held her in his arms and swore that she would be his bride . . . just as soon as she was old enough!

But for now, there were more adventures to share and more lives to save in the beautiful kingdom.

And so the girl and her horse rode away into the sunlight.

*　　*　　*

The little girl breathed a contented sigh and snuggled into her father's deep chest. She kept her eyes tightly closed so that she wouldn't notice that the enchanted kingdom had vanished. She didn't want to see the dingy, cold room, lit only by a single naked light bulb. She wanted to ride her horse and not feel the fingers stroking upwards from her knee.

She was the raggedy princess; that was her life, in the meadow, with the flowers and Glory. This was only her waking nightmare, something to be endured until the next time her father breathed plumes of whisky and was 'in the mood' to take her to the enchanted kingdom. What came after wasn't so bad; it was better than the other bad stuff, when he hit her until she couldn't remember anything. It wasn't so bad because all the time that it happened, he would promise that, one day, she would really own Glory. He would be her own real-life horse.

Glory stayed with the raggedy princess throughout her childhood and one day, one wonderful glorious day, she was given a date when Glory would be hers. On her sixteenth birthday, he would be brought to the gate with a big yellow ribbon around his neck. That made the thing bearable for a few more years. It bought her silence.

They found out about him hurting her when he lost his temper and she was taken away. Glory went too, and the raggedy princess and her horse rode in the meadow and roamed the kingdom while the doctor spoke about detachment.

He wrote to her occasionally and there would always be a paragraph about Glory. This was her favourite bit. 'Have saved a carrot for Glory,' he would say. That meant that he was going to buy the horse, didn't it? He wouldn't save a carrot for a horse that wasn't coming one day, would he?

She was released from the care of the state three days before her sixteenth birthday.

On her birthday, she went to him. She had dreamed of this day since she was six years old, when Glory had first become real to her.

He wasn't tied to the gate when she arrived. No magnificent white stallion with a pretty yellow bow. Somebody must be delivering him. He would come. Today was the day.

Her father was drunk, and so she made him some lunch. She hadn't seen him in over five years, and yet he hadn't changed. She waited for him to mention Glory. Surely he must know it was her sixteenth birthday today. He'd never really known who she was, but that didn't matter as long as he had remembered to buy Glory.

'Dad?'

'Yes?'

'When's Glory coming?'

He laughed. He laughed until he hawked, and then he spat a huge length of cloying phlegm into the back of the open fire. It hung on the flue-pull like a malignant epiglottis swinging in a blackened throat. She watched it, transfixed.

'Them, psy . . . psy . . . psycho wotsits said you was nuts. It was a fairytale, you bloody fool. Don't you know that? It was just a story. Jesus. You are one stupid bitch, aren't you? It was just a story. Hey, and don't think you're staying here. I had enough of you when you were a whining kid. Go on, bugger off. I don't want you.'

The raggedy princess lay beside the still form of the beautiful white stallion. His chest was stained red from the spear that the black knight had killed him with. The black knight rode away on his black horse, laughing.

The raggedy princess hugged Glory and wept ten years of misery upon his neck.

And so she was alone.

167

I Didn't Hurt the Baby

I had to leave the farm.

I was jealous of Jenny, the daughter, and had pushed her off a wall into the path of the tractor. I intended to kill her and hadn't thought further than that. I didn't consider consequences much. I wanted to be their little girl and there was already one daughter too many sitting on the old farm gate. Pam had given Jenny five presents for her birthday and I only got one. It wasn't my birthday but I still got a present so that I wouldn't feel left out. I did, though. They sang Happy Birthday to Jenny and she got to wear the nicest dress. I hated her.

Jenny wasn't run over but I was finished.

My next foster home was a disaster. It was in Preston. The house was big and the people were well-to-do. I can't remember their names but they had two kids around the same age as me, and a baby.

I know what I did to Jenny would never curry me any favour, but I swear I didn't do what I was accused of at that place. I was a bitch as a kid, but I didn't do that.

After what happened to Jenny, nobody believed me about anything. Even my social worker gave me hell for it. I swear I did not hurt that baby. I've never lied in this diary and now, thirty years later, if I had done it I would come clean and write it off as me being a screwed-up kid. I didn't do it. And I'm still bitter that I was accused. I wouldn't do that. I could happily have killed the two older kids, but I liked the baby.

They hated me. They heard my social worker telling the foster carer to just keep an eye on me around other kids. I suppose that's where they got the idea. They were horrible. It was the cuckoo in the nest syndrome again. At first, I tried to make friends with them but it was obvious that it wasn't going to happen. They were always trying to get me into trouble. In those days, it wasn't difficult with my temper. I expect they thought that if they got me into enough trouble, I'd be sent away.

The foster carer ran a nursery and had half a dozen kids on her books. I loved little kids and babies, and, if it wasn't for the other two, I might have been happy there. It was unfair because the parents believed everything that the little bastards said. It began with breaking things; ornaments and vases, toys, personal stuff that meant something to her. They had never done anything destructive before, so of course it had to be me.

At first, she tried to understand but was patronising to the point of sickly. She told her kids that I'd never had nice things and didn't understand how we have to look after them. She tried to make me apologise. I wouldn't. I'd done nothing wrong. She said that if I did it again I would be punished. Of course it happened again, and again, and again, and again. I'd be made to stand in the corner facing the wall and while she wasn't looking the kids from hell would smirk and sneer at me until I lost my temper, attacked them, and made things worse.

After this early success, they started to hit me. My sense of justice was high so I hit back—and some. They'd scream and holler and the bruises would be there to dob me in it and I'd be in trouble again. The husband had done his share of child psychology classes and was an expert on abused kids. He didn't like me. He wanted to get rid of me there and then. After all, I was bashing his little angels to a pulp. I was dangerous. I was fighting a losing battle and the kids had already won. All they needed was one final victory, but it had to be something good.

The baby was sleeping in his pram in the nursery. The mother gave us breakfast and went to hang out the washing. The kids ate and left me alone.

The baby screamed. It was obvious that he was in trouble. I got up and ran to the nursery. The first scream went on for what seemed like an eternity without a breath being taken. The ones that followed were no less piercing or loud. He was lying on his back punching the air with his fists and kicking out his legs. I'd been told that I wasn't allowed to pick him up but he was distressed.

I ran to his cot, picked him up and hugged him to me. It was summer and I remember how sweaty his head was. I was holding him tight and shushing into his ear while stroking his head when the mother rushed in. I passed him to her; it had only been a matter of seconds.

He had an ugly raw bite on his cheek.

I did not hurt that baby.

The police and my social worker were called. I don't know if the case went to court, I think probably not, because I didn't have to attend. I was accused of biting the child and questioned. I said that it wasn't me. The other kids were never even spoken to. If I hadn't been a care kid, the police would have looked into it more thoroughly and asked forensics to make an imprint of the bite to find out whose teeth did it.

I felt that the world had let me down again. I was supposed to be the disturbed one and yet one of those horrible kids bit a baby.

The story has a bright side, get me Pollyanna.

I still hadn't been removed from my dad permanently; it was only a school holiday fostering. I was terrified about going back to him, but he backed me to the hilt. He said that I would never hurt a baby or an animal and that the accusations were ridiculous. That was the first and only time that my dad ever stood my corner and wouldn't have a word said against me. I really felt as though he loved me that day.

After that, there were other placements, all without children. I had fourteen in all. The shortest lasted less than six hours; a middle class, middle-aged, churchgoing couple; do-gooders who cared more about their place in heaven than the kids they were supposed to be helping.

I don't know where this place was but I know that it was a long way from home. I'd been ill on the way there. I still felt sick when we arrived and I had a bad headache. I was ushered upstairs to get myself ready for dinner. I said that I wasn't hungry and asked that I be excused from the meal. They'd invited guests to join us for dinner. She told me that I was expected to sit at the table and try a little of everything.

I was embarrassed. I didn't talk if I could possibly avoid it, already at the beginning of my eating disorders and my five-year phase of being mute. Each new placement was a nightmare, having to sit at strange tables with strange people and being expected to eat in front of them. The woman decided that I would eat, or God help me.

The table was lavishly set with good crockery and fine glassware. I felt suffocated. My dad brought me up to have good table manners. He was fanatical about it.

As each dish was passed to me, I took it and put a tiny amount on my plate. The woman would take the dish from me and spoon a great heap on top of the bit I'd given myself. The last dish was cabbage. I didn't like cabbage and told her so. I probably added at least three pleases too many in an attempt to ingratiate myself.

She gave me the sixties lecture about the starving kids in Africa, droning on about her Christian duty and how good she was for taking me in. Highlighting my poverty, she humiliated me by criticising my father, saying that I'd probably never seen a cabbage before. She said that I didn't know what good food was.

Nobody was going to slag my dad off like that. He was a fantastic cook and often forced me to eat cabbage. It was as though I had been taken over by a demon. I didn't think about what I was going to do. It was just reactionary. It just happened.

As she droned on, I didn't even realise that I was still holding the dish of cabbage. I let fly and a gasp went out from every person sitting at that table, me included. I was more surprised than they were. The bowl hit her and soggy cabbage emptied over her head. Luckily, she wasn't badly hurt and the bowl smashed on the floor, spreading glass all over the room.

She sat in silence, allowing her brain to fully process what had just happened. The cabbage clung to her hair in tendrils. She looked like Medusa. Her lap was full of wet, smelly cabbage.

And then she screamed and cried. It was probably the most traumatic thing that had ever happened to her.

Jan, the social worker, was called but at such short notice a new placement couldn't be found for me.

I had my very first taste of a children's home that night. It was only for a few days until she found somebody else brave, or stupid, enough to take on a heathen like me. Jan was losing patience with me and spent much of her time lecturing and shaking her head.

Peterson House was a place of horrors. I was told that the staff were abusive and the kids were hardcore bad. The House was the last step before borstal, which was still in existence in those days. The children were feral and aggressive, some already on drugs, some young alcoholics. Some had been abused and some were abused-abusers. Life for the kids in that place was hard.

Thankfully, I was barely there long enough to find out first-hand just how hard it was.

The Great Escape

When I started work, I went from being the golden girl in the refuge, their shining star, to being a pain in the bum. I was flouting the way that things were done. I refused to hang my head, stoop my shoulders and slouch around like a victim, which was unheard of, but to have the audacity to go out and get myself a good job and have a social life? Well, broken girls don't do that. There's no rule in the handbook to cover it.

On the sixteenth of June, I got back to the refuge at ten past nine at night. I'd been on call all evening and at work since eight. I was exhausted and just wanted a shower and bed.

I'd been asking the refuge about my bill since I started work just over two weeks ago. They kept telling me not to worry, that it would be capped and I'd only have to pay a percentage of the five hundred and odd pounds a week costs. One member of staff even told me that they had special dispensation to waive the rent and living costs for one working person, and I was the only resident who had a job.

I was buzzed in through the security doors and Jean, the refuge manager, was waiting for me. She'd stayed late.

Ever since starting work, they'd been shitty with me about stupid house meetings and freedom groups. As a resident, it was in my contract to attend both of these as part of my abuse recovery. I'd had a letter through my door telling me that I had to arrange time off work every Wednesday morning for the compulsory house meeting and again on Thursday afternoon for the counselling sessions. It was ironic that I was on a freedom course and yet they were using it to take away my freedom to work. Jean and I got into an argument in the foyer.

I told her that I hadn't been told how much I had to pay. She quite rightly said that it was because I was never there to speak to, and that she'd had to book overtime and stay late to meet with me. She was inconvenienced and annoyed. She handed me my bill.

Those people were great to me at a very low point in my life. They gave me somewhere to live when I had nowhere, but it was an institution with institutional rules and I'm not a person that fits in boxes.

In retrospect, I'm not sure if she looked terrified or smug when she gave me the bill, but she knew damn well that there was going to be a reaction.

For two weeks and one day's stay at the Hotel de Battered Femmes, I was expected to pay seven hundred and ninety-six pounds and eighty-three pence plus seventy-two pounds in service charges. I looked at the figures in disbelief. I couldn't afford that. I told her that every member of staff that I'd spoken to had told me that it would be capped and I wouldn't be expected to pay more than a hundred pounds a week.

I couldn't afford it.

She expected me to pay just short of nine hundred pounds, there and then. I told her that I didn't have it. She asked me when I would be paid and what arrangements I could make for paying the bill. She said that future bills would have to be paid in advance and not in arrears as people had done flits owing money in the past.

I was trying to save for a place; I was never going to get my own home if I was knocking up over five hundred quid a week in costs to stay at the refuge. My wage didn't cover it, never mind leaving me anything over to get to work, live a life and save for a house. Besides this, I'd had to work time in hand.

I said that I'd pay the service charge and I paid the seventy-two pounds, which left me broke and worried about petrol for getting to work.

I went into what I can only describe as a panic attack. I told her that I couldn't stay there another minute. I had to get

174

out. Every night spent there was another massive whack of money that I couldn't afford. The bill was rising; it was like a metronome in my head and with every tick another pound was added to the costs of being there.

'I'm leaving. I can't stay here.'

'What about the bill?'

'I'll pay it, every penny of it. I give you my word, but I can't stay here.'

'I can't let you go until this account is settled. You do understand that, don't you?'

'I'm going to Gemma's. You have her address. You have Phil's address and you have my work address. Do you really think I want you ringing my boss to say that you're from the battered woman's refuge and that I haven't paid my bill? I promise, I will pay you. I'll come back religiously every Friday and give you a hundred pounds until it's paid off. But I've got to get out of here tonight.' I meant it, too.

'I'm sorry, Harpie, I can't let you leave until this account is settled in full. Is there anybody you could borrow the money from?'

'No, of course not. I can't come up with almost a thousand pounds just like that.'

I can't remember the next five minutes. It's a blur but voices rose. She refused to let me leave and I told her that I'd call the police. It was false imprisonment. I was in a panic and I felt my temper rising. Some of the girls had congregated in reception and were listening in. The upshot was that she couldn't stop me leaving; I could go where I liked, but she had every power and the force of the law behind her to impound my belongings. She could stop me taking my laptop and my car, both of which I needed for work. I was behind security doors and metal gates. How the hell was I going to get out?

I went to my flat to pack. Gemma had started seeing her ex again and had chosen that one night, of all nights, to bugger off to Wales for a couple of days. I rang her and she told me to use my key to let myself in. Of course I could stay at hers. Hadn't she been telling me that for weeks?

She had.

'I can't stay at yours; they won't let me out, well, not with my workbag and my car anyway.'

'What you gonna do, mate?'

'I haven't a clue.'

'Ring Harry. See if he's got any ideas.'

'And what's he going to do? Bowl over like Mr T on a dirty great bulldozer and ram the gates down? Gemma, they're refusing to let me take my car. I can't get to work tomorrow.'

What happened next was an amalgamation of two forces that came together and worked beautifully. The Great Escape had nothing on me.

I rang Harry and, predictably, he said to get the director in—a male—and he'd smash his face in. He ranted and raved and then he calmed and went into thought-mode. 'We'll get you out through a window.'

'Harry, I can leave through the door, numpty. I just can't take my car with me.'

He thought some more and came up with a plan that was nothing short of genius.

I told him that it'd never work but what the hell. I'd give it a go.

I packed my work bag, making sure that I had some clean knickers and my toothbrush. I dressed in the clothes that I'd be wearing for work the following morning, and then I started packing all my possessions into black bin bags. At that point, I thought that I had no choice but to leave them behind. The important thing was getting my work stuff and my car out so that I could get to work.

While I was packing, divine intervention called and the second part of my breakout plan knocked on the door. It was

Cidre and Connie, two of the hard-arsed women. We were mates and they'd heard what had happened in reception.

'It's fucking out of order, that is, mate. That's some mashed up fucking shit. You know what I'd do? I'd bottle her in the fucking face and put all her winders through. Let's slash her tyres, see how she likes being fucking grounded. Its fucking oppression of the weakest, that's what it fucking is. I'd take it to my OAP, I would. I'd take it to the House of Fucking Parliament.'

Cidre was more thoughtful. She's a bright, intelligent lady who had flown an abusive arranged marriage. I explained Harry's idea and she came up with a plan that worked in conjunction with his.

Everything went crazy. I had three of the girls in my flat helping with wild, disordered, mad packing. It took me weeks afterwards to find anything. Somebody went to round up the lasses. Only one terrified woman out of all twenty-three flats was too scared to help. Kids were woken up and pulled from their beds. Cidre knew how to outwit the cameras in the communal halls and corridors. Soon, all the kids were in one flat with a single resident looking after them.

Now it was my bit. Harry was on standby so I walked calmly into reception. I smiled sweetly at Jean and told her how badly I'd overreacted. I apologised for losing my temper and told her I'm a hot head but I'd had time to think and cool down. Of course it was stupid leaving that night. I'd make arrangements to pay my bill that week and I'd give a week's notice and leave the following Friday. I told her my flight plan had been a knee-jerk reaction. After all, I had nowhere to go.

All the time I was talking to her, I was backing up and subtly leading her across reception until she was clear of the desk and away from the bank of monitors. I told her that I had to go out for an hour.

I knew she wouldn't believe me. She wasn't buying it and wouldn't let me take my car. I reasoned with her that I had to go and stuck to the ridiculous story that Harry had fed me.

The girls went into action. They'd made a human chain along the corridor and down two flights of stairs and were passing all of my belongings along the chain, across the smoking area and over the fence—thank God my karaoke gear made it in one piece. Two women were on standby in the park to stack it neatly on the free side of the fence to pick up if the rest of move went to plan. In less than ten minutes, they'd emptied my entire flat and got every one of my belongings to safety.

Jean still wouldn't let me out of the gates with my car.

This is where good fortune comes into play. That night and the following night, Robbie Williams was playing in Manchester. I stuck to the story even though it sounded stupid, even to me. I was cursing Harry.

'Jean, I've got to go or somebody could be seriously hurt. My company's doing the security for the Robbie Williams concert tonight and they underestimated how many fans would turn out. It's pandemonium on the streets outside the venue and they need another fifty guards there in the next hour before the concert ends. Ten thousand more people are going to hit the streets and it's wild out there. I've got to go.'

Bang on cue, Harry rang pretending to be my harassed boss. I excused myself and stepped discretely away from Jean but put him on loudspeaker so that she could hear.

'Harpie, have you set off yet? I need you back here now, it's going crazy. If we don't fill this cover we're going to lose the contract. Where the hell are you?'

'I'm setting off now, Alec. I've just had a small problem here.'

'A small problem? Harpie, Robbie Williams is on his third bloody encore and they can't keep him on stage much longer. Half a million'—he exaggerates too—'teenage girls are going to get crushed if you don't get these guards out so they can clear the venue. It's going to be Hillsborough all over again. Get here now.'

'I'm on my way.'

I looked at Jean. She was convinced. I gave a nervous glance towards the cameras but the girls, apart from the two watching my stuff in the park, had long since scattered. Jean buzzed me out, telling me to ring if I was going to be home any later than midnight and she'd let the night staff know to relax the rules and let me in.

I walked calmly out in my pinstriped dress and stilettos with my hair pulled into a tight corporate bun. Connie was slouching on a post by the car park and she high-fived me as I walked past. I was dying to give her a hug but couldn't in case Jean smelled a rat. If she realised that I was leaving, there's no way she'd open the gate.

My heart was in my mouth as I got in my car and turned it round to face the gate. I had my laptop in the bag beside me. The gate was opening an inch a second as I sat there, drumming my nails on the steering wheel, watching the gap widen. Every second that passed I expected the motion to reverse and the gate to shut again.

I gave Connie a toot, but not until I was clear of those gates. And I was free. I drove around the corner and into the park. The girls had moved my stuff up to the main gate and helped load it into my car.

I've since sent two payments of a hundred pounds to the refuge, but I still owe well over six hundred. I can't pay it at the moment as I'm out of work and I know that Jean will think that I've let her down. Once I get another job, I'll resume the payments until I've paid every penny that I owe them.

I'll never forget the sisterhood of those women. All bar one came together for a common cause, to help me. It was the ultimate feeling of girl power. I worried about how much trouble they'd be in when the staff watched the cameras back, but Connie said they couldn't chuck them all out and not to worry about it.

We were all different characters but bound by a common reason for being there. We'd all suffered in our own way, which formed a silent bond and made for an uncharacteristic defence of each other, surpassing creed, colour or class. I'd have done the same for any one of them.

And that is what I call an escape.